# WHITBY

ALEX BROWN

No part of this book may be reproduced in any form or by any electronic or mechanical means, including information storage and retrieval systems, without written permission from the author, except for the use of brief quotations in a book review.

Whitby is a work of fiction. As fiction, every single name, business entity, character, geographical location, happenings, events, and incidents in this novel are entirely a product of the author's vivid imagination. Resemblances to the names of anyone living or dead and or anything depicted is entirely coincidental.

Text Copyright © 2026 by Alex Brown

Distribution Rights © 2026 Open Kimono Publishing, LLC

All rights reserved.

Published in the United States

Open Kimono Publishing, LLC

Edited by Nicoletta M. Cosentino

Library of Congress Cataloging-in-Publication Data

Names: Brown, Alex, author.

Title: Whitby / Alex Brown

Description: First Edition. | Thornton, Colorado:

Open Kimono Publishing, LLC

ISBN Identifiers:

Description: First edition.

Identifiers:

Hardcover ISBN: 978-1-961763-83-8

Paperback ISBN: 978-1-961763-84-5

E-book ISBN: 978-1-961763-85-2

Subjects: LCGFT: Fiction—Gothic fiction. Fiction—Horror fiction. Fiction—Science fiction.

Classification: PS3602.R44545 W48 2026

Library of Congress Control Number: 2026930456

LC ebook record available at https://lccn.loc.gov/2026930456

Our books may be purchased in bulk for promotional, educational, or business use. Please contact your local bookseller or Open Kimono Publishing at info@openkmedia.com.

www.openkimonopublishing.com

www.x.com/openkimonopub

www.facebook.com/openkimonopublishing

## CHAPTER 1
# DISCREDITING

We're all escaping something. Some of us don't even know what it is exactly, but we feel it. It claws relentlessly at the backs of our necks, draining the life from us, stealing our will to live. It's the voice that whispers to stop—to give up—that no more can be done. One more second, another minute, one more labored breath—it's unbearable. It's more than I can bear. It's sheer insanity, expecting different results while trudging through the same relentless grind. We're all beyond reproach, and maybe, we're all insane.

I have the luxury of knowing what I'm escaping. Success. That's the thing about reaching the top: it marks you. You wear an invisible scarlet "A" on your chest for all to see. People look at you like you're something more than human, yet also somehow less. No one tells you about the stigma, the crushing expectations that come with success. It's like carrying a backpack full of bricks, with society expecting you to bear it silently, gracefully. It's true what they say: be careful what you wish for, because you just might get it.

My wish was granted with the success of my novel, *Behind the Morning's Glass*. It won the Pulitzer Prize. Critics called it "The novel of the century... A riveting, insightful look into the ambitions of the human psyche and the sacrifices we make to achieve the unattainable... a masterful work by H.A. Hopes." It's absurd, really, how something as insignificant as words on a page can take on such weight when they resonate with people's emotions. If you can make someone feel, if you can give them belief—true belief—you give them the one thing everyone desperately searches for: hope.

Hope is fleeting, though. People cling to it with every ounce of strength because, without it, we have nothing. Hope is the engine that drives humanity—hope for a better tomorrow, a better job, a better life. But hope isn't a strategy; it's more like a religion. A thin veil to keep our minds from devouring themselves in the darkness of reality. I've seen the power of hope and the hollow void left when it's gone. When someone loses hope, it's unmistakable. Their eyes turn into black holes, their pupils consuming the light. They walk the earth like a living postmortem, their soul drowned in a sea of despair.

I know because I've been there. I was a gaunt shadow of a man—a failed writer, a failed father, a shell of a human being. That was when I wrote that cursed novel. *Behind the Morning's Glass*. Even thinking about it makes me sick. I poured everything into it, every vile and hopeless truth I had. It was my surrender—a hateful diatribe against life itself. And yet, it resonated. It succeeded.

For decades, I'd tried. Query after query, rejection after rejection. I sent countless emails, spent endless hours on the phone, only to be ignored. Then, when I'd given up—when I succumbed to that disease—I wrote something from the depths of my despair, and the world ate it up. I sent the book to one last publisher, not expecting anything. It was supposed to be my final rejection. But it wasn't.

Six weeks later, the call came. They loved it. Negotiations began, literary agents swarmed, and soon, twenty-four million copies had sold. And there I was, with more money than sense. Book tours, interviews, appearances—it was relentless. I had achieved what every writer dreams of. I'd made my break. But success has claws, too, and its grip is iron.

In every interview, I dreaded the same question: "What are you working on now?" The truth was a gnawing void. There was nothing. The disease had written the book—not me. My publisher demanded another bestseller, but I knew I couldn't deliver. I had sold my soul to write the book. There was no going back. You either keep the machine running, or it grinds you to dust. So, I left.

I went to Whitby.

Whitby was a place I visited once in college. During a study-abroad program in Manchester, I spent a weekend there, alone. It was the kind of place that stays with you, a town where the air carries the scent of salt and the faint tang of fish and chips. The cobblestone streets were ancient, worn smooth by countless steps. It had an eerie comfort, a sense of insignificance that made you feel oddly at peace. High above the town, Whitby Abbey loomed—a crumbling monument of stone and shadow, its ruins watching over everything.

Coming back now, the town was as I remembered. The salt air, the cobblestones, the Abbey—it was all the same. Yet it felt different, darker. The Abbey's silhouette wasn't just a ruin this time. It was a presence, oppressive and unyielding, like the book come to life. This was where I'd chosen to escape, though I wasn't sure what I was looking for—or running from exactly.

I rented a small, damp room above a pub, The Endeavour, overlooking the harbor. I was drawn to it because of the name and the location. It seemed fitting. It seemed, in this exact moment, like it was exactly where I was supposed to be. It's as if the iron in my blood was attracted to the very soil here, in this very place. I felt a sort of refuge in the fact that here, I had a sense of anonymity and I let it settle over me. No one recognized H.A. Hopes here. I could disappear. At least I hoped. The flight from Denver to Manchester was long; I had to have a layover in Newark. The Newark airport is a miserable experience. Definitely worse than the almost two-and-a-half-hour drive from Manchester to Whitby. I hate driving but I hate flying even more. Nonetheless, it's all a means to an end. A necessary evil that we all must endure. I've always wondered about necessary evils and the true validity of their existence. This is what is circling around in my head during the drive to Whitby. I booked a chauffeur, who promptly picked me up from the airport. My driver, Mr. Roberts, seems like a nice guy. He's astute enough to recognize the fact that conversation is not on my priority list. He knows that I want to be left alone. I feel like he may even feel the same unmistakable feeling himself. Still, the seemingly mundane evils of society are an ever-present jest. The fact that I can book a stranger in a different country to pick me up in a nice car from a particular destination at a set time and deliver me to a destination of my choice—all for a price. I wonder if the evil, the price itself, is worth it. Being honest, I'm not sure. It's a bitter pill that we all must swallow. Our work, our toils, our sufferings—or at least the sufferings we choose—do we really have a choice? It's just like the disease, does it choose us or do we choose it? There are more questions than answers in this life it seems, and we don't have enough time to answer most of them. I stare out the car window thinking about all of this and am pleasantly surprised by just how green everything is. It's something that I had forgotten about, something that I took for granted. We never give thought to these kinds of things until they're literally right in front of us, consuming our worldview. It's another reminder of the rat race that we find ourselves drowning in. The sheep are painted in foreign colors, as if mocking nature itself. I can't tell if it's for identification, health monitoring, breeding management, or some combination of the three. Either way, I can't shake the feeling that I'm one of them—a sorted sheep. Everybody has a name, everybody has a number. In the end I think we all die alone; it's just a choice of what we choose to die from. What a luxury—to have a choice. See, this is exactly why I dread monotonous periods of travel; it pushes me into my own mind. A devil like me, the one who sets expectations and lies about realities that perpetuate the disease.

I finally arrived at The Endeavour, a sour red-brick building with a weathered facade, crowned by an imposing sign that read "The Endeavour" in gold-embossed letters. Overlooking the harbor and proudly claiming to be dog- and family-friendly—what more could I possibly ask for? At sixty pounds a night, it was well within my price range, at least for now. I would need to find more permanent accommodations, but it didn't get any better than this. The fact that the first floor housed a pub was not just practical and charming—it felt like home. After thanking Mr. Roberts, with a fifty-quid tip and a nod, I gathered my bag and made my way to the front door.

As I stepped through the door of The Endeavour, I was immediately greeted by the mingling scents of ale and salt air, a comforting reminder of my first visit to the town. The small reception area felt more like an extension of the pub than a formal hotel lobby, with its dark wood paneling and the faint hum of conversation from patrons. The woman behind the counter smiled warmly, her accent unmistakably Yorkshire, adding to the charm of the place. I smiled and remarked, "Checking in—Hopes, H.A." She paused briefly while looking at her computer.

"Ah, Mr. Hopes, welcome to Whitby. Your room is on the third floor, room thirty-three. The Wi-Fi password is here on this pamphlet. It looks like we have you staying seven nights. Should you need anything, anything at all, just let me know. My name is Julie."

She handed me a set of brass keys, their weight fairly substantial, and pointed toward a narrow staircase tucked in the corner. Again, I gave her a nod and a smile—I could tell it wasn't well received; she was expecting more words from me. As a man of few words, I held my ground, confident with the nod. She continued, "Room thirty-three, just up the stairs," gesturing with a practiced ease that made me wonder how many travelers had been directed here before me. Again, I extended a nod and a fake smile. The check-in process was refreshingly simple—no barrage of forms or forced small talk. Instead, there was a quiet understanding, a sense that this wasn't just a transaction but an exchange of trust. At this very moment though, I wasn't in need of a room—I was in need of a drink.

I bellied up to the bar, acting as if I'd been there a thousand times before. The waiter caught my eye. I uttered, "A Guinness, please." He gave me a nod. I liked this place already. I watched him as he poured my drink; he filled it about seventy-five percent full then let it sit. Another good sign—they obviously knew how to pour a proper pint. After it had appropriately settled, he finished the pour and carried it across the bar to me.

I lifted the glass, its dark, almost black liquid crowned with a thick, creamy head of foam, the hallmark of a well-poured Guinness. The weight of the pint felt solid in my hand, grounding me for what felt like a small ritual. The rich aroma wafted upward—roasted malt, a hint of coffee, and something faintly nutty. As I took my first sip, the foam brushed against my upper lip, velvety and smooth. The liquid itself followed, cooler than I expected, sliding over my tongue with a perfect balance of bitterness and subtle sweetness. It's like tasting depth itself—the roasted barley hits first, bold and earthy, followed by a creamy smoothness that lingers at the edges of my mouth. I swallowed, and the flavor evolved, leaving a slightly dry finish, like a whisper asking me to take another sip. The experience wasn't just drinking a beer; it was savoring a piece of history, a taste as timeless as the pub around me. It was dark, mysterious, and comforting all at once. For a moment, everything else faded away. This was the escape I had been looking for.

My peace was suddenly bitten into by another thick Yorkshire accent. "Are you American?"

I could tell it was a woman's voice, rich and smooth, with a cadence that carried both curiosity and challenge. I refrained from looking left, the direction the voice was originating from, and answered, "Yes... but don't hold it against me."

The voice continued, dipping into a teasing lilt. "Well, that's for me to decide, isn't it?"

Her tone sent a current through me, both playful and

commanding, and I felt my resolve falter. Slowly, I turned my head, and when my eyes met hers, the world shifted. Her skin glowed with an almost hypnotic warmth, as if kissed by the deepest shades of sunset. It had a flawless smoothness that made me wonder if even silk would envy its texture. The light from the pub's dim chandeliers danced across her cheekbones, sharp yet inviting, and her full lips were painted with a color that seemed just bold enough to match the intensity of her gaze.

For a moment, I forgot how to speak. Her eyes—dark and endless—pulled me in, holding a depth that suggested she'd already seen through every facade I might try to put up. There was something inherently magnetic about her, something that both warned and invited me to step closer.

"And what," she asked, her voice softer now, yet no less commanding, "brings you here, to this little corner of the world?"

I cleared my throat, trying to steady myself. "I needed a change of scenery," I said simply, though even I knew that explanation barely scratched the surface.

Her lips curved into a slow, deliberate smile, and she tilted her head slightly, as though she was deciding whether to push for more. Instead, she extended a hand toward me, her fingers long and elegant. "I'm Elise," she said, her name rolling off her tongue like the whisper of a secret.

I took her hand, noting the oddly cold but inviting chill of her touch. "H.A. Hopes," I replied, suddenly feeling the absurdity of offering my pen name instead of something less... official.

"Ah, a man of mystery," she said, her smile deepening. "Or maybe just a man with secrets."

Her words hung in the air, laden with an energy that

felt electric. My pulse quickened as I met her gaze again, and I knew that whatever I said next would determine the outcome of this interaction.

"I'm an open book," I said, my tone deliberately light.

Her interest seemed piqued as she leaned in slightly, her voice dipping just enough to draw me closer. "So, what brings you to Whitby?"

I allowed myself a smile and met her gaze. "You."

Her lips curled into a slow, smile, one that seemed to radiate both amusement and intrigue. "Oh really?" she asked, her tone teasing yet inviting.

"Really," I replied, my voice steady, though my pulse quickened in the pause that followed.

The air between us felt charged, the kind of moment that was pregnant with possibility, daring one of us to take the next step. I wondered if she felt it too, or if this was all just a game she was effortlessly winning. Judging by her expression—a perfect mix of curiosity and challenge—I suspected it was both.

Her smile deepened, and there was a flicker of something playful in her eyes as she leaned back, crossing one leg over the other. "Well," she said, her voice smooth and laced with flirtation, "it seems I've been looking for you too."

The words hung in the air, deliberate and suggestive. My brow arched slightly, unsure whether she was teasing or testing me. "Oh? That's quite the coincidence, considering we've never met."

"Are you sure about that?" she countered, the corner of her mouth quirking up. Before I could respond, she continued, "I work at a little flower shop just up the hill. Maybe you wandered in one day and didn't even realize it."

I shook my head, smirking. "Trust me, I'd remember if I had."

"Hmm." Her finger traced the rim of her glass absentmindedly as she studied me, her gaze sharp yet inviting. "So, if it's not flowers you're here for, then what are you running from? Or should I say, who?"

I laughed softly, shifting in my seat. "That's a bit forward, don't you think?"

She shrugged, unabashed. "It's Whitby. No one ends up here without a reason." Her eyes narrowed slightly, as if dissecting me. "But you don't have to tell me, not yet. What do you do then, Mr. Open Book?"

I hesitated. The words caught in my throat, but her gaze held steady, and I knew she wouldn't let this go. Finally, I sighed and admitted, "I'm an author."

Her reaction was instant. Her head tilted slightly, curiosity lighting up her features, and then it clicked. "Wait," she said, her voice soft with growing excitement. "No, it can't be... *Behind the Morning's Glass*? That's you?"

I nodded, reluctant but unable to deny it. "That's me."

For a moment, her expression was unreadable, caught somewhere between awe and disbelief. Then, her smile returned, brighter and warmer than before. "I loved that book. I've read it at least twice. It's..." She paused, searching for the right words. "It's like it knows you better than you know yourself. Like it's been reading your thoughts before you even had them."

Her enthusiasm unnerved me, though I couldn't say I was surprised. The book always elicited strong reactions, and hers was no exception. But still, her praise didn't sit comfortably; it never did.

"That's high praise," I said cautiously, my tone even.

"It's honest," she replied firmly, leaning closer. "Why didn't you say so earlier? I would've never guessed."

"Maybe because I'm not that person anymore," I admitted, my voice quieter now. "Or maybe because I'm not sure I ever was."

Her smile softened, and there was something in her eyes now—sympathy, perhaps, or understanding. Whatever it was, it pulled me in despite myself.

"Well," she said after a beat, her voice lighter again, "I guess I'll have to stick around and figure out who you are now, won't I?"

Her words caught me off guard, but I couldn't help the smile tugging at my lips. "You're awfully persistent for someone who sells flowers."

"And you're awfully elusive for someone who writes about the truth." She raised her glass, and the moment lingered, charged with something unspoken but undeniably present.

I raised mine in return, and as our glasses clinked softly together, I realized there was no escaping this encounter—not that I wanted to.

I raised a hand to catch the bartender's attention, signaling for another round. "Another for me," I said, then glanced back at her. "And one for you too, if you're staying."

Her lips curled into a sly smile as she leaned back, clearly enjoying the gesture. "Well, I suppose I can't say no to that."

The bartender set down a fresh pint in front of me, then turned to her. "What'll it be?"

"Surprise me," she said smoothly, her eyes never leaving mine. There was a flicker of mischief in her gaze, like she was daring me to figure her out.

As the bartender moved to pour her drink, she tilted her

head slightly, studying me. "You're full of contradictions, you know," she mused. "The quiet, brooding type who still manages to be generous."

I shrugged, smirking. "Maybe I'm just trying to keep you guessing."

She laughed softly, a low, melodic sound that drew the attention of the few patrons nearby. "Oh, I'm guessing, all right. But don't worry, I'll figure you out eventually."

The bartender placed her drink—a deep amber ale—on the counter, and she lifted it with a nod of thanks. We clinked glasses again, this time with a shared ease that felt both natural and electric.

"To chance encounters," she said, her voice dipping into that dangerous flirtatious tone again.

"To Whitby," I countered, meeting her gaze over the rim of my glass.

As I took another sip, I couldn't help but notice how easily the moment settled between us, like it had been waiting to happen all along.

She swirled the amber ale in her glass, her eyes catching the dim light like pools of mystery. After a brief silence, she leaned forward slightly, her voice dropping to a near whisper. "Have you seen the Abbey yet?"

I nodded, taking a sip of my drink. "I have. It's impossible to miss. Hard to forget, too, with how it looms over the town."

Her lips quirked into that enigmatic smile again, her gaze holding mine. "But have you seen it at night?"

I paused, her question hanging in the air. "Not yet," I admitted. "Why? What's different about it at night?"

Her smile deepened, and there was a glimpse of something unspoken in her eyes. She set her glass down deliberately, leaning in just enough that I caught a faint trace of her perfume—a subtle, intoxicating blend of something floral and rich. "You need to see it at night," she said, her voice soft but insistent.

Her words were laced with something I couldn't quite place—urgency, maybe, or intrigue. Either way, they hooked me.

"What's so special about the Abbey at night?" I asked, trying to keep my tone casual, though I could feel the pull of her presence.

She tilted her head, studying me like she was deciding how much to reveal. "The Abbey... it's different under the moon. It's like it takes on a life of its own. There's a kind of magic to it, a beauty you can't see during the day." Her voice dipped lower, each word deliberate. "I could show you."

The offer lingered between us, its weight undeniable. I knew I should hesitate, question the sudden intimacy of her suggestion. But I didn't. I couldn't.

"When?" I heard myself asking, the word escaping before I'd had time to think it through.

Her smile widened, triumphant but still cloaked in that enigmatic charm. "Tonight. Midnight." She traced the rim of her glass with a fingertip, her eyes never leaving mine. "Meet me by the steps leading up to the Abbey. You won't regret it."

For a moment, the room seemed quieter, the hum of the pub fading into the background. There was something in her gaze that made it impossible to refuse, as if saying no would be denying gravity itself.

"Midnight," I repeated, the word feeling heavier than it should.

She lifted her glass and clinked it lightly against mine, her smile softening just enough to seem genuine but still holding that undercurrent of something more. "I'll see you there," she said, her voice a promise, a lure I was already ensnared by.

As she leaned back, finishing the last of her drink, I knew I should be wary. But instead, all I could think about was the way her words felt like a thread pulling me closer, toward something I didn't yet understand but couldn't bring myself to resist. She set the empty glass down gently, her fingers lingering on the rim for just a second before she stood. Her movements were unhurried, deliberate, like she knew I was watching and was in no rush to leave the stage. She didn't look back right away, her steps carrying her through the pub with an elegance that seemed out of place in the warm, rustic chaos of the room. But just as she reached the door, she paused. The cool night air spilled in as she pushed it open, her hourglass figure silhouetted against the dark. She turned then, glancing back over her shoulder, her eyes catching mine with that same unreadable intensity. Her lips curved into a soft, glowing smile, the kind that felt like both an invitation and a dare.

And then she was gone, the door swinging shut behind her.

I remained seated, staring at the spot where she had disappeared, my thoughts swirling as if she'd left some kind of spell in her wake. There was an ache in the air where she'd stood, a pull I couldn't quite explain. My glass sat untouched on the bar now, my mind too entranced to care about finishing it.

"Midnight," I reminded myself aloud, the word feeling heavy and electric all at once. Whatever it was about her—her voice, her presence, her mystery—it was already pulling me in, and I knew I wouldn't resist. I suddenly realized that my luggage was still sitting untouched, and I hadn't even been to my room yet. Shaking off the daze she'd left me in, I decided it was time to get myself sorted. Midnight would come sooner than I thought, and with the clock already nearing nine, I knew I needed to be ready.

As I made my way upstairs, the stairs creaked underfoot, each step a reminder of the building's age and character. My room was small but inviting, with a window that offered a stunning view of the harbor's lights bleeding in the night. The walls carried the faint scent of fresh linens, and a teapot sat waiting on a small wooden desk, accompanied by a selection of biscuits.

From the moment I walked in, The Endeavour didn't feel like a hotel—it felt like a retreat, a place where time slowed down just enough to savor the little things. The pub below hummed with life, but up here, it was just me and the quiet pulse of the harbor. It was a sanctuary disguised as a red-brick building. It wasn't the Abbey that called—it was Elise. Her presence lingered like the devil of seduction, weaving itself into my thoughts, her voice soothing with an allure I couldn't shake. Something in Whitby had shifted, and now it felt like she was the center of it.

I didn't know what it was about her—why her smile felt like a puzzle I was desperate to solve, why her gaze seemed to cut through everything I thought I knew about myself. All I knew was that she wasn't just someone I'd met by chance. She was something more.

Something was waiting for me, and it wasn't the town or its crumbling ruins. It was her. Elise. Creeping at the edges of my thoughts, pulling me in with every word she'd spoken, every glance she'd stolen.

We're all escaping something. The question is, what happens when what we're running from turns out to be what we're running toward?

## CHAPTER 2
# MIDNIGHT

The clock on the nightstand glows with an ominous insistence—11:37 p.m. The seconds tick away, louder than they should be, like they're counting down to something monumental. I rub my eyes, heavy with the weight of jet lag, but the thought of Elise pierces through the fog like a blade. Tired as I am, I know there's no chance of sleep now.

I force myself upright from the edge of the bed, my legs stiff from the flight and the long drive to Whitby. At thirty-one years old, I'm starting to feel the weight of my years. My body aches for rest, but my mind is alive with curiosity, adrenaline, and something else—an enthrallment I can't explain. I lean forward, elbows on knees, staring out the small window of my room. The harbor glimmers faintly in the moonlight, its calm waters reflecting fragmented pieces of the night sky. The world outside looks quiet, but I can feel the pull, an invisible string tying me to the steps of the Abbey—and to her.

The room feels colder now, though I don't remember turning off the heater. I grab my jacket, shrugging it over my shoulders with a groan. A glance in the mirror tells me I look as exhausted as I feel. My eyes are bloodshot, and I remark aloud to myself, "You look like shit." But something deep inside myself tells me it doesn't matter. Whatever this night is, it isn't about appearances. It's about something else entirely.

I slip the brass key into my pocket, the weight of it comforting. The floor creaks beneath my boots as I make my way down the narrow staircase, my breath catching briefly as I pass the pub. It's quieter now, the earlier hum of conversation reduced to a low murmur. A couple of patrons linger near the bar, but no one spares me a glance. Good. I don't want to explain where I'm going—or why. I catch the unmistakable musk of cigarettes as I near the front door—a stomach-turning comfort. There's something oddly grounding in the realization that some things, no matter where you are in the world, never change.

Stepping out into the night, the crisp air bites at my face, a stark contrast to the warmth of the pub. The streets are nearly deserted, the cobblestones slick with a faint sheen of dew. The town feels different now, cloaked in the dark of night, its edges blurred by the moonlight. The Abbey looms in the distance, its jagged silhouette cutting into the sky like broken teeth. I hesitate for a moment, stuffing my hands into my jacket pockets as I take in the scene. It's quiet, almost too quiet, the kind of silence that feels alive. The kind that watches.

The sound of my footsteps echoes softly as I start walking, each step carrying me closer to the promise of something unknown. I replay her words in my mind: Midnight. Meet me by the steps leading to the Abbey. You won't regret it.

There's a strange confidence in her voice, one that both

intrigues and unsettles me. Who is Elise? Why does it feel like she knows something about me that I don't? Why exactly am I so attracted to her—a complete stranger? It doesn't make any sense, but at the same time it feels as wrong as it is right. Like all the pieces in the universe's puzzle align—everything fits in this exact moment.

The walk through the city to the Abbey steps feels unfamiliar, a distorted path I'm certain I've taken before but can't seem to recall. The soft glow of my phone's GPS lights my face, guiding me through streets that seem both known and strange, as if the town itself has shifted in my absence. My legs protest with every step, a dull ache spreading through my calves, but I press on. The closer I get, the sharper the air feels, as if the atmosphere itself is changing. My breath escapes in visible puffs, each one laced with a faint sense of anticipation. The empty streets amplify the eerie stillness, their silence pressing in on me like a held breath. I brush off the unease—after all, it's just a Wednesday night. A Friday would paint a completely different picture, the town alive with chatter and movement, drunks and jubilation—a stark contrast to this quiet, forgotten moment. With no one else around, it feels like it doesn't exist—like a dream. I don't want to wake up.

Finally, I reach the platform where the one hundred and ninety-nine steps to the Abbey begin. The Abbey looms above me, its ruins bathed in pale moonlight. The broken arches and crumbling walls seem to glow faintly, almost as if they're alive. I pause, catching my breath, scanning the darkness engulfing me for any sign of her.

The stillness is unsettling. My pulse quickens—not from the climb but from the creeping thought that I might be alone. I glance over my shoulder, half-expecting to see a figure lurking around a corner. The eerie quiet of the night amplifies every sound—the rustle of the wind, the distant crash of waves—each one making me question if it's Elise approaching or someone else entirely. What if this is some elaborate setup? A way to rob tourists? The thought twists in my gut. Was I too eager to trust her smile, her charm? My hand instinctively tightens in my jacket pocket, brushing against the cool metal of my room key as if it could be some sort of protection.

Seconds seem to stretch into minutes, and doubt begins to take root. Maybe she isn't coming. Maybe I've been a fool, drawn into the romantic allure of her words, only to find myself standing here—waiting, vulnerable. Or worse, maybe this is how people like me get killed.

The Abbey looms above like a silent witness, its jagged silhouette casting ominous shadows on the stone below. I shake my head, trying to dispel the paranoia, but the unease doesn't leave. I tell myself it's just my imagination, but still, my eyes dart between the darkness and the ghostly glow of the steps. Where is she?

And then I see her.

Elise emerges, rounding the corner of the buildings, her figure illuminated by the silvery glow of the moonlight. She's draped in something dark, the fabric flowing around her like liquid, embracing her every movement. Her posture is relaxed, her steps unhurried as she approaches me with an almost ethereal calm. Her head tilts slightly upward in acknowledgment, and as she draws closer, I see it—a slow, knowing smile spreading across her lips, a smile that sends a shiver cascading down my spine.

"You came," she says, her voice cutting through the stillness like a blade through silk.

"Of course," I reply, though my voice sounds weaker than I'd like.

She steps toward me, her movements impossibly poised, her eyes glinting with something that feels like more than just moonlight. "You're tired," she observes, her tone soft but teasing.

"Jet lag," I admit, running a hand across my bald head. "But I'm here."

Her smile widens, and for a moment, she just looks at me, as if she's trying to see past the surface. "Good," she says finally. "Because the Abbey is different at night. It breathes."

I glance up at the ruins, the jagged edges of the stone stark against the sky. "Breathes?"

She steps closer, close enough that I can feel the faint chill radiating from her. Her voice drops to a near whisper, intimate and compelling. "You'll see."

And just like that, I know I'm already in too deep.

## CHAPTER 3
# ST. MARY'S CHURCHYARD

As we crest the final step—the one hundred and ninety-ninth—the world seems to end, but in a stillness that's palpable. The town below glimmers faintly with the refrain of each unnatural light. I take it in for a second before it's replaced by the open expanse of the cliffside and the haunting presence of St. Mary's Churchyard. The Abbey looms even larger now, its jagged stone spine visible to my naked eyes up close. I feel as if I could touch it, but it's still a bit of a walk away. The silence here is deeper, the kind that presses against your ears and makes you feel small in the face of something far older and greater than yourself.

I pause, catching my breath, my pulse still racing—this time from the climb and the sheer magnitude of where we are. Elise, however, is calm, her steps as elegant and unhurried as before. She stands ahead of me, her dark figure blending into the night, the folds of her skirt rippling gently in the breeze.

"Aren't we going to get in trouble for being up here?" I ask, my voice lowered as if the night itself might overhear.

She glances over her shoulder, her lips curving into that familiar, enigmatic smile. "Trouble?" she repeats, her tone light and teasing. "There's no one here to stop us."

Her confidence is unsettling and reassuring at once. I shove my hands into my pockets, glancing around the empty churchyard, the leaning gravestones scattered like forgotten sentinels. The thought of being caught lingers in the back of my mind, but Elise seems utterly unbothered, her steps carrying her toward the Abbey with an ease that feels almost otherworldly. Still, it gives me a cheap thrill—one I can't walk away from.

"Come on," she calls softly, her voice cutting through the stillness like a thread pulling me forward.

I follow, the sound of my boots crunching on gravel stark against the quiet. The Abbey gates are locked, the large iron bars casting long shadows across the ground, but Elise doesn't stop. Instead, she moves to a section of the fence that's slightly lower, her movements deliberate and graceful as she climbs over. I hesitate, looking back toward the steps as if expecting someone to appear and stop us. But no one does.

"Elise, are you sure—"

"I'm sure. You are too," she interrupts, her voice steady as she turns to face me from the other side of the gate. "Trust me."

It's those last two words that do it. Those two words have ruined my life before. Against my better judgment, I grip the cold iron bars and pull myself over, landing awkwardly on the other side. She stifles a laugh and offers her hand to steady me.

Together, we step into the heart of the Abbey.

The ruins feel alive, their tired arches cutting long, bold stretches of darkness across the ground that seem to shift with the moonlight. The air here is colder, sharper, carrying a stronger tang of salt, as if the place itself breathes with its own quiet vitality. The wind stirs suddenly, brushing against my exposed head, and I instinctively pull up my jacket's hood. Elise walks ahead, her steps deliberate, her head tilted back as her gaze locks onto the skeletal remains of the towering structure above us. It's almost as if she's never seen the Abbey at night before, though I know she has.

"It's beautiful," she murmurs, her voice reverent.

I glance at her, watching the way the light carries gently across her face. "It's... haunting," I say, unsure if I'm describing the Abbey or the woman before me.

She turns to me, her expression soft yet intent. "Haunting can be beautiful," she says simply.

For a moment, she's silent, her eyes tracing the lines of the ruins—the way moonlight filters through the empty windows and falls across the stone floor. "It breathes," she says finally, almost to herself.

I frown slightly. "You keep saying that. What do you mean?"

She steps closer, her movements slow and deliberate, as if she's considering how best to show me. "Here," she says, taking my hand and guiding it toward her breast.

Her hand rests lightly over mine, pressing it against her, against the rise and fall of her breath. Her chest is cool—startlingly so—the chill sinking into my palm.

"It's cold," I remark, my voice hushed.

She smiles faintly, her tone casual. "It's the night. It's cold."

Her gaze holds mine, and for a moment the world narrows to just the two of us. "What do you feel?" she asks softly.

I swallow, my thoughts scattered, her proximity crushing any attempt at clarity. "I feel…" I pause, the words slipping through my grasp like smoke. "I feel… alive. Like the Abbey itself is alive."

Her smile deepens, her eyes glinting with something that feels like understanding. "Exactly. It breathes."

"You're right," I murmur, my voice barely audible over the wind. "The Abbey does breathe at night."

She doesn't reply, but her smile lingers—a quiet triumph in its curve. The air between us shifts, charged with something I can't name. Standing there beneath the towering arches, moonlight spilling over her, I know I've crossed a line. Whatever this is—whatever she is—I'm completely caught.

Elise steps closer, her gaze steady and unwavering as she reaches out, her fingers brushing my cheek. Her touch is cool, startling at first, but the chill fades beneath the intensity of her presence. She doesn't hesitate, pulling me toward her, and before I can process what's happening, her lips meet mine.

They're cold—colder than I expect—but the sensation barely registers. The softness of her lips, the way they move against mine—it's all-consuming. The cold doesn't matter. Nothing matters but this moment, this impossible, undeniable connection.

I kiss her back, the rest of the world fading into the ocean just beyond the steep cliffs of the Abbey. There's nothing I've ever wanted more than this—than her.

Elise.

## CHAPTER 4
# THE LURE OF THE NIGHT

The world around me feels different now, as if the Abbey itself has exhaled and drawn me deeper into its grasp. The cold night air bites at my eyes, drawing unwarranted tears, but the chill is nothing compared to the fire Elise's kiss left behind. My thoughts are a mess—tangled between desire, curiosity, and the nagging sense that I've just crawled into something I will never be able to crawl out of.

Elise steps back, her gaze steady and unreadable. Her lips curve into a faint, satisfied smile, as though she knows exactly what I'm thinking. "Don't cry," she says, her voice teasing. "This is a moment you'll want to remember." The moonlight catches the angles of her face, illuminating her deep brown eyes. They seem to hold the entire night within them, sharpening her beauty into something almost inhuman, almost too perfect. I'm more than transfixed, more than captivated—I'm entranced.

I answer, "I'm not. It's—it's just the wind."

"Sure... See—you feel it now, don't you?" she asks, her voice soft but laced with a power that pulls at me.

"The Abbey—or you?" I manage, though my voice feels far away, as though I'm listening to myself speak from somewhere else.

She tilts her head slightly, as if amused by my answer. "We're one and the same," she flirts, her eyes locking onto mine. "It calls to some of us louder than others. It's why you're here, whether you realize it or not. This moment—it's forever."

Her words hang in the air, weighty and cryptic, and I can't decide if she's leading me deeper into something I'll regret or saving me from it. My heart pounds in my chest, a rhythm that feels both too fast and eerily in sync with the strange pull of the Abbey around me. She extends her hand again, not to pull me closer this time, but to lead me. Her movements are haunting, her footsteps silent as she turns toward the steps. "I have something else to show you," she says, her voice carried by the wind. "Something you need to see."

"What else could there be?" I probe.

"Something more—something you will never forget."

She leads me down the steps, holding my hand at first to guide me before slipping away toward the steep steps.

I ask again, "Where are we going?"

She stops her descent briefly and quips right back, "Is it important?"

I admit, "You're right, there's no place I'd rather be."

She smiles at my words, a flicker of amusement crossing her face before she resumes her descent, the folds of her dress flowing like liquid. I follow close behind, my steps steady as the steep stone staircase winds downward. The town below begins to unfold again, its lights scattered like jewels against the dark canvas of the night. The sounds of the sea grow fainter as the cobblestones beneath our feet become smoother, leading us away from the cliffs and into the heart of Whitby.

Elise moves with an effortless grace, her figure illuminated in brief flashes by the dim streetlights we pass. The narrow streets are quiet now, empty of the daytime bustle, and the silence of the town feels almost sacred. The old buildings loom over us, their weathered facades bearing the weight of centuries, each one a story I'll never know. This is the town I remember.

We make our way down Church Street, the ambient glow of amber streetlights reflecting faintly off the glossy cobblestones. Elise doesn't look back at me, her focus forward, but her presence commands me to keep following. There's an invisible tether between us now, something I can't see but feel pulling me closer to wherever she's leading.

At the bottom of Flowergate, she slows her pace, the faint glow of a sign catching my attention: The Little Angel. Its weathered lettering is lit ever so faintly by the light pouring out of the pub's windows—a stark contrast to the surrounding darkness. The sound of distant laughter seeps through the heavy wooden door, and I catch the faint aroma of alcohol—whiskey—and warmth, a comfort I didn't know I needed until now.

Elise stops just before the door, finally turning to face me. Her expression is lighter now, though her eyes still hold that unfathomable depth. "Here we are," she says, her voice low but carrying a weight that makes the simple statement feel anything but ordinary.

I glance at the pub, then back at her. "Why here?" I ask, my voice steady, though my curiosity presses harder.

Her lips curve into that familiar small, knowing smile. "You'll see. Everything starts and ends here—with me," she says simply, stepping forward to push the door open. Yellow light spills out, illuminating her face for a fleeting moment before she starts inside.

I pause. "Wait—do you smoke?"

"Only when I'm on fire," she jokingly responds. "Why—do you?"

"I'm trying to quit, but if we're going to have a drink..."

Before I finish my sentence, she continues, "Well then, smoke 'em if you've got 'em."

"I don't have any. Like I said, I'm trying to quit."

Still in the doorway, she doesn't hesitate. "That's a bad habit—but I'm worse." She calls out to a man smoking out front. "Hey, can I bum a smoke?"

He shrugs his shoulders. "Sure."

She nods to me, and we walk over to the man. Standing in front of the pub, he looks as though he's been carved out of the plaster facade itself. His figure is hunched slightly, his shoulders drawn up against the cold. A cigarette hangs loosely between his fingers, its ember glowing faintly in the dark. His eyes are tired, half-lidded, and framed by the kind of lines that come from years of worry and hard living, marked with a clear intoxication. His jacket—dark and fraying at the cuffs—hugs his thin frame, and his boots are caked with the grime of too many days working out in the mud. As Elise and I approach, his gaze lifts, meeting hers with a glint of curiosity but no real urgency. He looks like the kind of man who's used to being asked for smokes, favors, or maybe just directions, and he's already resigned to the request.

He extends the pack of cigarettes to her. She takes it and remarks, "For my friend too?"

"For you—anything," he replies.

I feel a coil of jealousy crawl down my spine before I take one. "Thanks," I say, insincerely.

"Cheers, mate. Joke is on you," he says.

I take the cigarette from my mouth. "What?"

He repeats, "Joke is on you—these things are bad for you, mate."

Elise shrugs her shoulders and nods. "He's not wrong."

"I know," I relent. What can I do?

Elise takes a long draw from her cigarette. Exhaling, she relents, "This is disgusting—but it scratches that itch."

Candidly, I agree. "I hate it. Can't stand it. The things we do to kill ourselves, huh?"

"Life's grotesque pleasures. Tell me about it."

Curious, I press, "So what exactly do you do in a flower shop?"

She exhales. "I make arrangements—bouquets and such. Weddings, funerals, anniversaries—you name it."

"I hate flowers exactly because of that," I say.

"Because of what?"

"Because they smell like death. Funerals, funeral homes, hospital rooms without hope—flowers are death. I hate it."

Her lips curve downward. "That's a dark way to look at it."

"It's the only way I can. I cannot stand flowers. No offense."

Elise nods. "That's not romantic at all. That's actually the antithesis of romance."

I quickly realize my mistake and try to take it back. "Well... maybe I..."

She interrupts me. "Stop. I like it—it's your truth. That's hard to get from people—their truth. Everybody is so inauthentic to get what they want. I like that you're not.

You're real, you don't come across that all the time. You're just like in your book, Behind the Morning's Glass—you're authentic..."

I cut her off abruptly. "Don't say that. I'm embarrassed that you even read it. That book... I wish I never wrote it."

Genuinely curious, she pushes. "What? Why? What are you talking about? It's an amazing book! How could you not be proud of something like that?"

I hesitantly try to explain. "Because... the book wrote itself, it's not me..." I drop my cigarette and snuff it out with my shoe. "I'm going to need a drink if we're going to talk about this shit."

She flicks her cigarette. "I thought you'd never ask."

I follow her in. The door closes behind me with a soft thud. Inside, the pub is alive with a hum of conversation and the clink of glasses, the smell of old wood, musk, perspiration, and flowing beer wrapping around me like a disgustingly calming blanket.

Elise has already moved toward a small table in the corner, her movements deliberate yet unhurried. She takes a seat at the table, a keg soldered to a round stainless steel tabletop. She turns to me, gesturing toward the bar and calling out, "A cider, please!"

I nod and head to the bar, weaving through the close-knit crowd. The bartender, a middle-aged man with salt-and-pepper hair and a weary but friendly face, surprisingly notices me before I reach the counter. His sleeves are rolled up, revealing forearms marked with faded tattoos, and he moves with the efficiency of someone who's been pouring drinks for decades.

"What'll it be?" he asks, his voice low but audible over the din.

"Cider for her," I say, gesturing toward Elise without looking back, "and a pint of Guinness for me."

The bartender pauses as he reaches for a glass, his gaze flicking over my shoulder toward where Elise sits. He hesitates for just a moment too long, then looks back at me, his expression subtly shifting—curiosity mixed with something else I can't quite place.

"You with her?" he asks, his tone casual but carrying a weight I can't ignore.

"Yeah, why?" I respond, raising an eyebrow.

He exhales slowly, wiping his hands on a towel draped over his shoulder. "Just... be careful with that one," he mutters, almost too quietly to hear.

"What do you mean?" I ask, leaning in slightly, my curiosity piqued.

He shakes his head, as if he's already said too much. "She's... different. Comes in here now and then, always with someone new—no offense. Don't know much about her, but... let's just say she's good at making people forget themselves."

"Forget themselves?" I repeat, unsure if I'm more confused or intrigued.

He shrugs, his eyes darting toward her again before refocusing on me. "You'll see. Just don't let her pull you in."

I glance back toward Elise, who's sitting casually at the table, her chin resting lightly in her hand as she watches me. "Fuck you—no offense," I reply, trying to sound unaffected as I hand the bartender cash.

He nods, his expression neutral again as he slides the cider and Guinness across the bar toward me. "Good luck," he says under his breath as I turn to leave, and though his tone is light, the words settle uncomfortably in my chest. I'm as angry as I am offended.

I make my way back to the table, the drinks in hand, and set them down carefully. Elise's eyes gleam as she picks up the cider, her fingers brushing the glass delicately.

"Everything alright?" she asks, her tone sweet but with a hint of amusement, as if she's enjoying the exchange she couldn't possibly have overheard.

"Yeah," I lie, sinking into the seat across from her. I take a long draw of my Guinness, the rich, bitter taste grounding me for a moment. "The bartender seems... like an asshole."

She raises her drink to her lips, feigning innocence. "An asshole?"

"About you," I say bluntly, watching for her reaction.

Her smile widens slightly, the edges of it curling into something almost predatory. "Oh, I'm sure he did. People always have their opinions, don't they?" She takes a sip of her cider, her gaze never leaving mine. "But tell me—do you believe him, or do you believe me?"

The question hangs between us, loaded and impossible to answer honestly. "Is that even a real question?" I take another drink, letting the silence stretch just long enough for one of us to break. Knowing the first one to talk loses, I look into her deep brown eyes. She subtly laughs.

I win.

"That's what I thought," she says, her voice low, followed with a wink.

And just like that, the warning from the bartender feels both distant and dangerously close, tangled up in the electric pull of the woman sitting across from me.

I gesture toward the bartender. "Do you know that guy?"

"I know everybody," she remarks as she sets down her cider. She continues, "He's an ex-boyfriend of mine—but don't hold it against me."

I smirk. "If he's your ex-boyfriend, why did you take me here? Are you just trying to make him jealous?"

Elise's laugh is soft, almost musical, but there's a sharpness to it that makes me wonder if I've struck a nerve. She leans back slightly, the curve of her neck jeering and almost threatening. "Jealous? You think I'm the kind of woman who'd waste time on petty games like that?" Her voice is smooth, almost too smooth, but there's a flicker in her eyes—amusement, deflection, or maybe both.

I hold her gaze, letting the moment simmer. "I don't know what kind of woman you are," I admit, setting my pint down with deliberate care. "You're a bit of a mystery."

She tilts her head, considering me. "Good," she says simply, leaning forward again and resting her chin on her hand. "But to answer your question, no. I didn't know he worked here, and I'm not trying to make anyone jealous—least of all you. I don't need to."

Skeptical, I frown. "You sure about that?"

She rolls her eyes, finishing the last of her cider in one smooth motion. "Do you really think I'd waste a second thinking about an ex while I'm sitting here with you?" Her voice is sharper now, more direct, as if daring me to doubt her sincerity.

I shrug, trying to appear nonchalant, but the truth is her words hit harder than I expect. "Alright," I say finally. "Prove it."

Her smile returns, softer this time, almost teasing. "Prove it?" she repeats, as if tasting the words. She sets the empty glass down on the table with a deliberate clink, then stands, her movements exact and commanding. "Fine," she says, holding out her hand. "Let's get out of here."

I hesitate for a moment, glancing toward the bartender, who's pretending not to watch us but failing miserably. His jaw tightens slightly when Elise's hand lingers in the air, waiting for me to take it. Part of me wonders if this is a bad idea, if leaving with her is crossing some line I don't fully understand. But then again, wasn't I already past that line the moment I followed her here?

I take her hand. Her grip is firm, her fingers cold against mine, and she pulls me to my feet with a confidence that feels almost magnetic. Without another word, she leads me toward the door, weaving through the crowd with an ease that makes it seem like the entire room parts for her.

As we step outside, the cool night air wraps around us, sharper now after the warmth of the pub. The streets are quieter than before, the hum of the town reduced to a faint murmur in the distance. Elise glances back at me, her expression unreadable but her eyes glowing in the dim glow of the streetlights.

"Now," she says, her voice low and edged with a challenge, "let me show you who I really am."

She begins to walk, her hand still holding mine, guiding me through the dimly lit streets of Whitby. In this moment, my love for this city is reignited. It's as if I can pick any dream I want. Suddenly, my senses come back to me. I hesitate for a moment, pulling slightly against her hand.

"Where are we going?" I ask, my voice quieter than I intend and noticeably vulnerable.

She glances over her shoulder. "Somewhere warm," she says simply, her voice carrying a playful edge that makes it impossible to resist.

I follow her steps. The streets grow narrower, quieter, until the faint hum of society is nothing more than a memory behind us. It's not until I catch the glimmer of keys in her hand that I realize where she's taking me.

"Your flat?" I ask, the words slipping out before I can stop them.

She doesn't respond right away, only glances back at me again with that same smile that holds more secrets than answers. "Do you mind?" she asks, though her tone suggests she already knows the answer.

I shake my head, caught between disbelief and anticipation. "No," I admit, my voice attempting to sound confident. "I don't mind at all."

Her flat is tucked away in the lower portion of the long, connected row of Victorian-style apartments, a garden flat nestled against the earth, its entrance slightly sunken below street level. The pale stone facade of the building looms above, softened by creeping moss that clings to the facade and twists along the edges of narrow windows. The warm amber light of a streetlamp above reflects faintly off the glass, casting soft shadows across the uneven stone steps that lead down to her front door.

Her entrance is modest, marked by a navy blue door framed with dark wood, its paint chipped at the edges. A brass knocker shaped like an anchor gleams faintly in the low light, a touch of nautical whimsy in an otherwise understated space. Planters of overgrown greenery line the small landing before the door, their leaves glistening with dew. The garden flat feels secluded, almost hidden, as though it belongs more to the soil and roots than to the world above.

She glances toward the flowers. "Do they still seem like death?"

I shake my head as I follow her carefully down the stone steps, watching my footing as I dodge the scattered snails making their slow, deliberate way across the slick path. She stops at the door, turning to look at me.

"This is it," she says softly, her voice calm yet charged with something unspoken.

She slides the key into the lock and twists it, the heavy door creaking open to reveal a warm, inviting glow spilling out from within. The faint scent of flowers greets me, mingling with the earthy dampness of the garden. I pause for a moment on the landing, glancing back up the steps to the street above, where the light feels colder, farther away.

I lied. Flowers still smell like death.

"Come on, you're welcome here," she murmurs, stepping inside, her voice as smooth and compelling as ever.

I duck slightly as I step through the doorway, the low ceiling of the entrance adding to the cozy, secluded feel of her flat. The warmth of the space wraps around me, and I find myself momentarily overwhelmed—by her, by the flat, by the surreal intimacy of it all. The door closes behind me with a soft thud, sealing us into her world, a place that feels as rooted and alive as the garden it sits within.

She locks the door and pulls the drapes. "Red or white?"

I answer, "Red, definitely red."

"I knew I liked you," she remarks.

She flicks on a lamp, its warm glow casting a soft golden hue over the room, which feels as carefully curated as she is—cozy but full of quiet intrigue. The furniture is simple yet elegant, mismatched in a way that feels intentional rather than accidental. A green plush sofa, draped with a knitted blanket, sits against one wall, while the other is lined with shelves bursting with books, small vases, and a handful of dried flowers adjacent to a small television and fireplace. Everything about this space screams Elise—unexpected, inviting, and brimming with mystery.

"Make yourself at home," she says over her shoulder as she moves toward a small alcove off to the side, her silhouette disappearing behind the doorway. "I'll grab the wine—and change into something a little more comfortable."

Her words linger in the air, and for a moment, I'm frozen, unsure where to start. The intimacy of the flat feels overwhelming, as though I've been invited into a piece of her she doesn't share with just anyone. I glance around, my eyes catching on the small details—a stack of books on a nearby coffee table, the edges of their covers worn from frequent handling; a single fresh flower, stark white, standing tall in a slim vase; and a collection of postcards tacked to a corkboard on the far wall, each one bearing the marks of places she's been or dreamed of going.

I sink into the sofa cautiously, the plush fabric giving way beneath me. My hands rest on my knees as I lean forward, staring at the small fireplace across the room. It's not lit, but it adds to the room's faint inviting nature.

Elise reappears moments later, her steps light but deliberate. She's traded her dark, flowing attire for a pair of black shorts and an oversized sweater that somehow makes her seem even more radiant. Her hair is pulled back loosely, strands framing her face in a way that feels effortlessly perfect. She carries two glasses and a bottle of red wine, the label faded and nondescript, but the sight of it alone makes my chest tighten with anticipation.

"Comfortable?" she asks, her voice casual, though her eyes scan me as if she's assessing more than just my posture.

"Very," I say, though the word feels inadequate.

She sets the glasses on the coffee table, uncorking the bottle with a smooth motion and pouring the wine. The rich, ruby liquid pools into the glasses, the aroma wafting upward and mixing with the lingering scent of flowers, which is off-putting, but I cannot resist the situation. I cannot resist Elise.

She hands me a glass, her fingers brushing mine briefly, sending a shiver down my spine. "To tonight," she says, raising her glass slightly, her gaze locked onto mine.

"To tonight," I echo, clinking my glass gently against hers.

The first sip is smooth, the flavors deep and bold, a perfect match for the moment. Elise sits beside me on the sofa, tucking her legs beneath her as she leans back, the picture of ease. She studies me over the rim of her glass, her eyes gleaming with something unreadable.

"So," she begins, her voice playful yet laced with that ever-present undertone of mystery, "tell me—what does someone like H.A. Hopes think about all of this?"

"All of this?" I repeat, swirling the wine in my glass.

She nods, gesturing subtly around the room. "Being here. With me. Tonight."

I take another sip, the warmth of the wine spreading through me as I search for an answer. "I think," I say slowly, meeting her gaze, "that I've never wanted to be anywhere else more than I do right now."

She takes a slow sip of her wine, her eyes never leaving mine, before setting the glass down on the table. "Flattering," she teases, her voice light, though there's an edge of sincerity beneath it. Her British accent is as invigorating as it is attractive. "But I imagine someone like H.A. Hopes has a way with words."

I hesitate for a moment, the weight of her gaze pressing against me. The wine emboldens me, loosening the tight grip of my hesitation. "Actually..." I begin, setting my own glass down carefully. "There's something you should know."

Curiosity flickers across her face. "Oh? What's that?"

"H.A. Hopes... isn't really my name." The words leave my mouth with a quiet finality, as if I've just exposed something fragile. "It's just my pen name."

She tilts her head, studying me for a beat, her expression unreadable. "Really?" she says, her tone hovering somewhere between surprise and intrigue. "So, what's your real name, then?"

"Alex," I admit, feeling the weight of the truth settle between us. "Alex Brown."

Elise leans back slightly. "Alex Brown," she repeats, almost as if tasting the words. "It's... simpler than I expected. Less dramatic."

I laugh softly, the sound more nervous than I'd like. "Yeah, well, I figured H.A. Hopes sounded more... literary. More marketable."

"What's H.A. stand for then?" she presses.

I laugh. "It's short for Huge Ass Hopes—H.A. Hopes."

Her eyes narrow slightly, but the smile remains. "That's priceless and practical," she says, laughing as though she's working through the thought herself. "I suppose it makes sense. Keeps a little distance between you and... all of this." She gestures vaguely, as if indicating the world beyond her flat.

"That's the idea," I say, shrugging. "When I wrote the book, I wasn't exactly in a place where I wanted my name —my real name—attached to it. It felt... safer, somehow. Like I could hide behind it."

She nods again, her expression softening. "I get it. Everyone has huge ass hopes," she says, surprising me with the quiet sarcasm and understanding in her voice. "It's like wearing a mask, right? People see the mask, but they never really see you."

"Exactly," I reply, meeting her gaze. "It's not that I don't want to be seen. I just... I don't want everything out there, you know?"

She picks up her glass again, swirling the wine thoughtfully before taking another sip. "Well, Alex," she says, her voice warm but teasing, "I suppose I should feel special, then. Not everyone gets to know the man behind the mask."

"Yeah," I say, my voice quieter now. "I guess so."

"I like Alex," she says, setting her glass down again. "It suits you."

"Better than H.A. Hopes?" I ask, leaning back slightly.

"Definitely," she replies without hesitation. "H.A. Hopes might have written Behind the Morning's Glass, but Alex is the one sitting here with me tonight."

The way she says it, so certain and without pretense, sends a quiet warmth through me, one that has nothing to do with the wine. For the first time in what feels like years, I don't feel the weight of the name I've carried. I just feel... me. And with her, in this moment, that feels like enough.

"You seem nervous," she says, tilting her head slightly as she studies me.

Trying to hide the knot tightening in my chest, I answer, "Maybe a little. But... I'm happy. I don't know why, but I am."

"Good," she utters as she places her hand on my thigh. "I want you to be."

Her touch is light but grounding, sending an unmistakable current through me. Her fingers are cool against the warmth of my skin, but her presence ignites something deeper, something I haven't felt in far too long. I meet her gaze, her deep brown eyes locking onto mine with an intensity that makes the rest of the world blur into insignificance.

She leans in closer, the space between us shrinking, her face so near I can see the faintest flicker of her pulse at her neck. "You're overthinking," she whispers, her voice low, soothing, and impossibly alluring.

"Probably," I murmur, unable to pull my eyes away from hers. "It's a habit."

"Let me help you forget," she says softly, and before I can respond, her lips brush against mine.

The kiss is tentative at first, her lips cool and soft, tasting faintly of wine. But it deepens quickly, her confidence coaxing me out of my hesitation. My hands find her waist, the fabric of her sweater smooth under my palms, and I pull her closer, needing to feel the reality of her against me.

Her hands slide up my chest, her touch deliberate yet gentle, as if she's memorizing every line of me. She moves with an effortless grace, her lips never breaking from mine as she shifts to straddle me, her knees resting on either side of my thighs. The weight of her, the rhythm of our breathing syncing, and the quiet hum of the world outside disappearing completely.

I trail my hands up her back, her sweater bunching slightly beneath my fingers as her movements grow more deliberate. I slip my fingers into her hair, tugging gently, and a soft sound escapes her lips—a sound that makes my pulse race and my thoughts dissolve. She leans back just enough to meet my eyes, her lips parted slightly, her cheeks flushed.

"You're not nervous anymore," she observes, her voice teasing but breathless.

"Not even a little," I reply, my voice lower now, steady with the certainty of the moment.

She grins, leaning in again, her lips finding mine with a

hunger that matches my own. Her hands explore my shoulders, my neck, the curve of my jaw, as if she's determined to leave no part of me untouched. I let myself get lost in her—in the warmth of her, the taste of her, the way her body fits so perfectly against mine. Time becomes meaningless, every second stretching and folding into the next as we lose ourselves in each other.

Her hands tug at the hem of my shirt, and I let her pull it off, the cool air brushing my skin for only a moment before her touch replaces it. Her kisses trail from my lips to my jaw, my neck, her lips soft but insistent, as though she's trying to consume every piece of me.

I reach for her sweater, my fingers trembling slightly as I pull it over her head. The sight of her leaves me breathless, her beauty unguarded and almost otherworldly in the warm light of the room. She leans into me again, her lips capturing mine as we move together, the world outside her flat completely forgotten. I gently pull at her shorts, and she helps them off. She traces her hand down my chest, to my belt, unbuckling it and taking it off. Her eyes lock with mine as she unzips my pants and takes them off. There's a sense of inevitability in the air, as if this moment was always meant to happen, as if we've been drawn to it by forces beyond our control.

As I hold her, feel her, lose myself in her, I know there's no turning back—not from this, not from her. Elise is everything I didn't know I was searching for, and in this moment, I'm hers completely. The whites of her eyes seem to disappear as her pupils dilate in sheer ecstasy. I have never wanted anyone more, never craved something more.

Her lips meet mine again with renewed urgency, and everything about her feels all-encompassing—her scent, her touch, her presence. It's as though she's consuming me, piece by piece, until there's nothing left but this moment, this connection, this raw, undeniable need.

Elise pulls back slightly, her breath mingling with mine, her face so close I can feel the warmth of it against my skin. Her hands trail down my arms, her fingers brushing my wrists as she takes my hands in hers and guides them back to her waist.

"You feel that?" she says in my ear, her voice trembling, not with hesitation, but with something deeper, something primal.

"Yes," I breathe, though I'm not sure what I'm agreeing to. I feel everything—her heartbeat, her skin beneath my palms, the quiet hum of something between us that words can't describe.

Her smile is faint but electric, and she tilts her head, her hair cascading over her shoulder as she leans in, pressing her lips to my neck. The sensation is enough to unravel me, to bring me further into her orbit. My fingers tighten around her waist, pulling her into me as her lips travel, exploring with an intensity that leaves me breathless. Her hands find their way back to my chest, her nails dragging lightly across my skin, and a shiver runs through me.

"You're mine now," she murmurs against my skin, her voice low and edged with something I can't place—possessiveness, maybe, or a warning. It sends a thrill through me, though I can't tell if it's excitement or something darker.

"I'm yours," I reply, the words spilling out without thought, without hesitation. I mean them. In this moment, there's nothing else, no one else—just her.

Elise pulls me closer, her body pressed against mine. The room feels warmer, the air heavier, as though it's holding its breath along with us. Time slows, stretches, and I lose myself completely in her—the rhythm of her, the taste of her kiss, the way her touch ignites every nerve in my body.

When her lips return to mine, it's softer this time, less frantic but no less intense. She cradles my face in her hands, her thumbs brushing lightly over my cheeks as if grounding me, tethering me to her.

"Alex," she calls, and hearing my name on her lips sends a rush through me, a wave of something I can only describe as need. "You have no idea what you mean to me. I'm going to finish—don't stop."

I want to ask what she means, want to understand the weight behind her words, but I can't find my voice. Instead, I keep going, pouring every unspoken question and emotion into her. Her response is immediate, her body melting into mine, her hands gripping my shoulders as though she's holding on to something fragile and fleeting.

The fire between us burns hotter, brighter, until it feels as though it will consume us both. I don't care. Let it burn. Let it take everything, as long as it leaves me with her.

Elise is everything—

## CHAPTER 5
# METICULOUS

I would've been more careful with my wanting if I'd known it could take shape and come for me. If I'd known they were more than idle words spoken blankly into the dark or drunken musings slipping through the cracks of lonely nights. But I wasn't, and now I find myself in Elise's bed, with no memory of how I got here.

The room is quiet, the kind of quiet that feels heavier than it should. Elise is beside me, propped on one elbow, her dark eyes fixed on me with a calm intensity. Her hair falls loosely over her shoulders, barely covering her breasts, framing her perfect figure, veiled by the sheets.

"Good morning," she murmurs, her voice soft but still carrying that low, enigmatic pull.

"Morning," I reply groggily, my throat dry as I shift beneath the covers. My body feels oddly stiff, like I've run a marathon without realizing it. There's a faint ache at the side of my neck, sharp but dull at the same time. I reach up instinctively to rub the spot but stop myself when I catch the way her gaze sharpens for just a fraction of a second before softening again.

"Sleep well?" she asks, her tone casual, but there's something behind her words, like she's testing the waters.

"I think so," I say, though my voice betrays uncertainty. The truth is, I don't remember falling asleep. The night feels like a puzzle, the edges smudged and pieces missing, and yet, looking at her, none of it feels out of place.

Elise doesn't press, just smiles softly and shifts out of bed, her confidence inescapable. "I'll make coffee," she says over her shoulder as she leaves the room. I watch her walk out wearing only her pink lace panties—a stark juxtaposition against her beautifully dark skin.

The moment she's gone, I sit up, the ache in my neck more persistent now. I press my fingers against the spot, wincing slightly at the tenderness. It's nothing, I tell myself. Maybe I slept wrong. Still, the faint pain lingers as I swing my legs over the side of the bed and stand.

Her flat is quiet, save for the soft hum of a kettle boiling in the kitchen. I spot a door slightly ajar and head toward it, hoping it's the bathroom. Inside, the light flickers on, bright and sterile, and I lean over the sink to splash some water on my face. When I glance up at the mirror, my breath catches me off guard. Two small, distinct puncture marks sit just above the curve of my neck, faint but unmistakable. The skin around them is slightly reddened, the marks themselves pale and precise, as if they've been there for hours. My fingers hover over them, brushing lightly, and a strange chill runs down my spine.

"What the hell?" I mutter to myself, leaning closer to inspect them. They don't bleed, don't ooze, but the placement is too perfect, too deliberate to be accidental. A bug bite? No. Too symmetrical. Too clean.

Before I can think further, her voice calls out from the kitchen. "Alex, are you okay in there?"

I snap back, my hand dropping from my neck as though the marks might disappear if I ignore them. "Yeah, just waking up," I reply, my voice steady despite the churn of unease in my chest.

I return to the bedroom just as she steps back in with two mugs of coffee, her smile as warm as the steam rising from the cups. She hands me one and sits on the edge of the bed, watching me closely as I take a sip.

"It's past noon," she says casually, as though she's announcing the time on a lazy Sunday morning. "I was thinking... why don't you take me to lunch?"

"Lunch?" I ask, still distracted by the marks on my neck. "Sure, where?"

"There's a pub near here that does a proper Sunday roast," she says, her eyes lighting up at the mention. "It's been ages since I've had one."

"Sunday roast?" I repeat, trying to match her enthusiasm. "Alright, sounds good."

Her smile widens, and for a moment, I forget the oddity of the morning. Elise has a way of pulling me into her, making everything else feel irrelevant, even the strange unease I can't quite shake.

"I'm going to shower first though—do you care?"

"Not at all," I answer. "Care if I shower after you?"

"Why don't you shower with me?" she says.

"Together?" I ask, my voice catching slightly, though the suggestion has already ignited a warmth beneath the surface.

She tilts her head, her dark eyes glinting with amusement. "Why not? Save time... water..." Her voice dips, teasing but soft. "And besides, it might be fun."

I swallow hard, my mind scrambling for a response, but my body is already moving, following her lead as she turns toward the bathroom. She doesn't look back, as though she knows I'll follow without question.

Elise reaches for the faucet, turning the knob with a practiced ease, and the steady sound of water fills the space. Steam begins to rise, curling lazily into the air as she steps back, her fingers brushing the hem of her panties before removing them.

I hesitate for a moment, caught between the surreal intimacy of the moment and the ever-present pull she has over me. She notices, of course, and turns to face me, her smile softening into something almost tender.

"You're overthinking again," she says quietly, her voice cutting through the steady hum of the water. "Just be here. With me."

Her words are simple, but they hold a weight I can't quite place. I nod, exhaling slowly as I step toward her. She reaches for my shirt, her fingers, already wet from the shower, brushing lightly against my skin as she helps me out of it. There's no rush, no urgency—just a quiet, unspoken understanding as I shed the last layers between us.

The heat of the shower envelops us as we step inside, the water cascading over our skin. The space is small, forcing us closer, and I find myself completely captivated by her—the way the water glides over her shoulders, tracing the curves of her body; the way her dark skin glows in the soft light filtering through the steamed-up glass. She's breathtaking.

Elise turns to me, her hands reaching for my shoulders as she steps closer. "See?" she murmurs, her voice barely audible over the sound of the water. "Much better."

Her fingers trail down my arms, her touch light and

deliberate, and I can't help but let out a soft laugh, the tension of the morning dissolving under her care.

"You make it impossible to think," I admit, my voice low.

"Good," she replies, as she leans in, her forehead resting lightly against mine. "Thinking ruins moments like this. Bend me over."

I do exactly that, embracing the way we fit together. The intimacy of the moment. It feels right, like this is exactly where I'm meant to be. Her hands move to my back, as she pulls me closer into her, and I feel the last of my hesitation fade away.

The water continues to pour over us, in this moment, it's just her and I, the quiet rhythm of our breaths mingling with the steady stream of water. It's not rushed, not frantic —it's deliberate, a sensation between us that feels both familiar and entirely new. Like its the first time for both of us.

Elise pulls back slightly, her dark eyes meeting mine with a gaze that holds onto me. "You feel it too, don't you?" she asks softly, her voice steady but laced with something vulnerable.

"Yes," I reply without hesitation, my hand brushing against her cheek. "I feel it."

Her smile widens, and she leans into me, her eyes fluttering closed for a brief moment. The shower continues to cascade around us, the heat of the water matching the warmth between us, and for the first time in what feels like forever, I let myself fully exist in the moment. Nothing else matters—not the marks on my neck, not the questions lingering in the back of my mind. Just her, just us, just this. I've never had better—I'm completely entranced. She moans, an exotic, inexorable call that carries through the room until she stops thrusting, pressing herself tightly against me, shuddering. "Fuck— did you finish too?"

I nod, "I couldn't help myself." She pulls forward and turns around, hugging me. She kisses me and gives me a playful slap, "Clean yourself up, you animal." She bites the tip of my right ear after her last word.

I finish showering and step out, the cold air of the bathroom biting against my skin after the warmth of the water. I grab a towel, wrapping it around my waist as I glance back at the fogged mirror. The faint marks on my neck catch my attention again, but I shake off the unease, telling myself it's nothing. Just a strange coincidence.

Elise stays in the shower, and I can still hear the water cascading softly behind me as I step into the bedroom. Her flat feels quieter now, the stillness wrapping around me like a blanket, yet my mind is anything but still. I dry off quickly, slipping into the clothes I was wearing yesterday. I feel inherently dirty without clean clothes, but it's my only option for now.

The sound of the water shuts off, and a moment later, she emerges from the bathroom wrapped in a soft, white towel. Her damp hair clings to her shoulders, tiny droplets of water tracing paths down her neck and arms. She moves with an effortless grace, crossing the room to her dresser, where she begins to pick out her clothes.

She doesn't say anything at first, just hums softly to herself as she pulls out a fitted sweater and a pair of jeans. There's something mesmerizing about the casual intimacy of the moment—watching her, knowing this is her space, her life, and I've somehow become a part of it, even if just for now.

She turns to me with a playful smile, her eyes glinting

with amusement. "You're staring," she teases, her voice light but warm.

"Can you blame me?" I reply, leaning back slightly with a grin. "You make it hard not to."

She laughs softly, shaking her head as she moves back toward the bathroom to finish getting ready. "Well, I hope you're hungry," she calls over her shoulder. "The Sunday roast at this place is worth it."

"I am," I reply, pulling on my jacket and slipping my phone into my pocket. "How far is it?"

"Not far," she answers as she reappears, now fully dressed, her hair tied loosely back, still damp and frizzy. She grabs a small umbrella from the corner of the room and flashes me a smile. "A short walk, but you might want to bring a coat. It looks like it's still raining."

I nod, pulling my coat fully on as she slips on a pair of boots. The casualness of the moment is comforting, but there's an undeniable energy between us—a connection I can't explain but don't want to question.

She locks the door behind us as we step outside into the cool, drizzly afternoon. The rain is light, more of a mist than a downpour, but she pops open the umbrella anyway, holding it above her as we walk side by side. The street is quiet, the faint sound of raindrops hitting the pavement the only thing accompanying our steps.

Elise looks over at me, unguarded. "You'll like this place," she says, her voice carrying a confidence that makes me believe her. "It's one of my favorites."

"I'm sure I will," I reply, matching her pace as the pub comes into view ahead, its lights cutting through the misty gray of the afternoon. For now, the questions in my mind can wait. Right now, it's just her and me, and that's enough.

The pub is charming, a quintessential English establishment nestled on the corner of a bustling street. Its stucco facade is weathered but inviting, with hanging baskets of wilted flowers swaying gently in the misty breeze. The sign above the door creaks slightly in the wind, proudly declaring the name of the establishment in faded script: Hales Pub.

Elise pushes the door open with ease, holding it just long enough for me to follow her inside. The unforgettable savory smells of roasted meat, ale, and the faint scent of a wood-burning fire burst alive in the air. It's warm—comforting, even.

She leads me toward a table near the window, where the light from outside mixes with the warm glow of the pub's interior. I can't help but notice the way she moves, with a quiet confidence that draws attention without trying. Heads turn as she passes, subtle but noticeable, though she seems utterly unaware—or unbothered.

We settle into our seats, the wood of the chairs creaking slightly beneath us. A waiter approaches, a notebook in hand and a friendly smile plastered on his face. The familiarity between him and Elise is immediate; his smile widens, and there's a flicker of recognition in his eyes.

"Elise," he greets her, his voice warm and casual. "Back again? It's been a minute, huh?"

She smiles up at him, leaning back in her chair with a relaxed ease. "It has, hasn't it? Life gets busy."

"It does," he agrees, then glances at me briefly before returning his attention to her. "Sunday roast?"

She tilts her head thoughtfully, then nods. "Yes, for both of us, please—and two pints of Guinness."

The waiter scribbles it in his notebook before looking at me again, his smile polite but curious. "I'm sorry, where are my manners? I'm Tanner—and you are?"

I pause for a moment, deciding what name to use or whether to use a name at all. "A friend," I say with a wink.

"Okay—friend..." he says politely before walking off.

"A friend?" Elise playfully mocks. She leans forward slightly, her elbows resting on the table. "He's nice, isn't he? I've known him for years."

"Another ex?" I tease, though my tone is light, and I can't help but smile.

She laughs softly, shaking her head. "No, just a friend. Believe it or not, I don't have a history with every man in Whitby."

"Well, that's a relief," I say, leaning back in my chair. "I'd hate to think I'm just part of a pattern."

Her gaze sharpens slightly, her smile turning into something more mysterious. "Oh, Alex," she says softly, her voice dipping into that familiar, seductive tone. "You're not part of a pattern. You're... different."

The words hang between us, and for a moment, I'm not sure how to respond. Her eyes hold mine, unblinking, and I feel the pull of her once again, that magnetic force I can't seem to resist.

Before I can say anything, the waiter returns with our drinks, setting them down with a practiced ease. "Food won't be long," he says, giving us both a quick nod before disappearing again.

I lift my pint, taking a sip and letting the cool, luxurious liquid settle on my tongue. Elise watches me, her pint untouched for the moment, as if she's studying me, waiting for me to speak.

"Well—what am I? A friend?" I ask finally, setting the pint down and meeting her gaze.

"No—you're mine. Much more than a friend... you and me—well, we are together," she says, her lips curving into a small smile. "I mean—if that's what you want. You said you were mine last night."

I shrug, trying to keep my tone light. "Well, maybe I am—would you like that?"

"No... I'd love that," she says simply, picking up her glass and taking a slow sip. "Because moments like this don't come around often. I've never met anyone like you, and I know I never will. You... you're one in a million. I want you. I want to be with you—I need to be with you."

Her words send a chill down my spine, but I don't let it show. Instead, I raise my pint again, clinking it gently against her glass. "To us!"

She meets my glass with hers without hesitation. "To us. To moments like this, chance encounters that restore our hope in humanity—in each other," she says, her smile widening slightly. But as she takes another sip of her Guinness, I can't help but feel that there's more to her words than she's letting on.

She doesn't let me get too caught up in the moment. Instead, her gaze shifts to my wrist. "Why do you wear that thing?" she asks suddenly, pointing toward my watch.

"What do you mean?" I counter quickly, glancing at it.

"It's... small," she says, her tone half-joking.

"Small? It's thirty-four millimeters. It's modest. It's old—it's from 1957. A rare watch."

"Let me see it," she says, gesturing for me to take it off.

I unclasp it and place it gently in her hand. She tilts it under the dim pub light, squinting slightly as she reads the dial. "Rolex—Oyster Perpetual... what's that mean?"

"Oyster means the case is water-resistant, and Perpetual refers to the self-winding movement. It winds itself whenever I move my wrist."

She examines it further, her brow furrowing as she reads aloud, "Stainless Steel, 1311879."

"That's the serial number," I explain, leaning forward slightly. "Like I said, it's old. And the reference is a 5552."

"Hmm." She turns it over in her hand, her fingers brushing the case back. "It's nice," she says finally, handing it back to me. "Not flashy, but... why?"

"Why what?" I say, clasping it back onto my wrist. Her curiosity feels oddly personal, as though she's trying to piece me together through the objects I carry.

"Why that watch? I imagine you could wear any watch you want—but you chose that one... why?"

I glance down at it, the polished steel catching the faint glow of the pub's lights. For a moment, I hesitate, the weight of her question heavier than I expect. "Well," I say slowly, "it reminds me of the impermanence of life. I was born in 1991—this watch existed long before I did. It's seen lives I'll never know, stories I'll never be a part of. Whoever owned it before me, they lived completely separate lives and now it's mine... for a while, at least. We're connected without ever even knowing that each other existed."

I pause, turning my wrist to admire the watch's quiet elegance. "It reminds me that I'm just a guest here. One day, I'll be gone too, and this watch will keep ticking, winding itself on someone else's wrist. It's a reminder that I'm impermanent—just flesh and blood in a world that keeps spinning long after I'm gone."

She leans back, studying me, her expression softer now, almost reverent. "That's... beautiful," she says quietly, her tone stripped of its usual teasing edge. "I didn't expect that."

"It's cheesy, I know," I admit with a faint smile. "But

that's why I wear it. It's a piece of history on my wrist. A reminder to live while I still can."

Her gaze lingers on me for a moment longer, and I can't tell if she's impressed, intrigued, or something else entirely. Then, finally, she smiles—a small, genuine smile that feels like its own kind of connection. "I think I get it now," she says softly. "It suits you."

I feel a strange comfort in being seen—not just by her, but by the world itself. It's intimidating but reassuring. I smile my doubts away. "Well—thank you."

"We're all just passing through—aren't we?" she says.

I nod. "I think so—but what do I know? I don't know everything," I admit candidly.

The waiter returns, balancing two steaming plates of Sunday roast. The rich aroma of roasted meat, crispy potatoes, savory gravy, and Yorkshire pudding fills the air, mingling with the pub's comforting musk of worn wood and faint hops. He sets the plates down carefully, his movements practiced but deliberate, as though he's placing something sacred before us.

"There you go," Tanner says with a warm smile, stepping back slightly. "Enjoy."

"Thank you," Elise says, her tone light but with a certain charm that seems to disarm everyone around her. Tanner's gaze lingers on her for just a moment before he nods and steps back, leaving us alone again.

I glance down at my plate, the food arranged with almost artistic precision. The golden brown of the roast potatoes contrasts with the deep green of the vegetables and the dark, glossy sheen of the gravy pooling around the meat. "Looks amazing," I say, picking up my fork and knife.

"It is," Elise says, already cutting into her roast. "You'll love it. There's nothing quite like a proper Sunday roast."

I take a bite, and she's right—it's rich and hearty, a comforting blend that feels like home, even though I'm far from it. The warmth of the food spreads through me, grounding me in the moment. Across the table, Elise eats with a quiet elegance, her movements unhurried, her expression serene.

"So," I say, joking between bites, breaking the silence. "Do you come here often?"

She looks up, a faint smile playing on her lips. "Not as much as I'd like. Life has a way of pulling you in all sorts of directions, doesn't it?"

I nod, swallowing another bite. "Yeah, it does. But it's nice to have places like this, where everything feels... steady."

"Steady," she repeats, as if testing the word. "I like that. Steady is good."

We eat in companionable silence for a while, the clink of cutlery against plates and the low hum of conversation from other tables filling the space. Outside, the rain taps gently against the windows, a rhythmic backdrop to the warmth inside. I notice how other silences like this would usually make me feel uncomfortable—like a gnawing at the back of my skull that I need to say something. I don't feel that here and now. It feels right, peaceful. I don't have to say a word and we completely understand each other. It's the first romantic silence I've ever experienced.

"You know," she says after a while, setting down her fork and looking at me with a thoughtful expression, "I think you're more steady than you give yourself credit for."

I raise an eyebrow, surprised. "Steady? Me? I don't know about that."

"I do," she says simply, her gaze unwavering. "There's something about you... something grounded. Like that watch of yours. You carry pieces of the past with you, but you're still here, in the present."

Her words catch me off guard, and for a moment, I'm not sure how to respond. I take a sip of my Guinness, letting the smooth bitterness settle on my tongue as I gather my thoughts. "Maybe," I say finally. "But I think it's more like... I'm trying to be steady. Doesn't mean I always succeed."

"That's enough," she says softly, her tone carrying a quiet conviction. "Trying is enough."

The simplicity of her statement feels profound, and I find myself nodding, the weight of her words sinking in. "Maybe you're right."

She smiles, and it's one of those rare smiles that feels completely genuine, like she's seeing something in me that even I can't see. "Of course I am," she says lightly, picking up her glass again. "Now, eat up before it gets cold."

I chuckle, shaking my head as I return to my plate. "Yes, ma'am."

As we finish our meal, Tanner returns to clear our plates, his friendly demeanor unchanged. "How was it?" he asks, his gaze flicking between us.

"Amazing, as always," Elise says, flashing him a smile.

"Glad to hear it," he replies, picking up the empty plates. "Anything else I can get you?"

"How about another round?" I say, glancing at Elise, who nods in agreement.

As Tanner walks away, Elise leans back in her chair, her eyes meeting mine. "Well?" she says, a playful lilt in her voice. "Did I deliver?"

"You did," I admit, smiling. "Best Sunday roast I've ever had."

She grins, her eyes sparkling. "Good. I'd hate to lose my reputation."

I laugh, shaking my head. "I don't think you could if you tried."

Her smile softens, and for a moment, the playful energy between us fades into something deeper. "Thank you for today," she says quietly. "For saying yes to this."

"For you—you're my only yes," I say.

She leans back. "Do you think you would ever move here? Would you get homesick?"

I pause, taking a long drink from my pint as I consider her question. "I could see myself living here—with you," I say, meeting her gaze. "I don't know what home is, really. But you... you're the closest thing I've ever felt to it. Here, now, with you—Whitby feels like my home."

I know my answer is a complete gamble, one that could either push her away completely or show that we're walking the same line, together.

Elise holds my gaze, her expression unreadable for a moment, as if she's carefully choosing her words. The pause stretches just long enough for me to wonder if I've said too much, if I revealed my hand too soon—but then she leans forward slightly, resting her elbows on the table.

"You're mine," she says, her voice steady and soft, her eyes holding a depth that leaves no room for misunderstanding.

Her words hit me like a quiet revelation, simple but profound. There's no hesitation, no pretense—just the truth, laid bare between us. For a moment, I forget to breathe. I nod slowly, my heart pounding as her gaze stays locked on mine.

"I'm yours," I reply, the words coming out before I even realize I've spoken them. They feel right, natural, as if they were waiting for this moment all along. And in that instant, everything else fades away—no questions, no doubts, just her and the unshakable certainty that this, whatever it is, is exactly where I'm meant to be.

Elise's smile softens, but there's a sharp, dark glimmer in her eyes, something I can't quite place—a secret, perhaps, or a promise. She reaches across the table, her fingers brushing against mine. The coldness of her touch grounds me, silencing the noise of my own thoughts.

"Good," she murmurs, her voice barely audible over the quiet hum of the pub. "Because this is just the beginning."

Her words linger, heavy with meaning I can't yet decipher. The room seems to fade around us, the world narrowing to just her and me, and the unspoken truth hanging between us: whatever comes next, there's no going back. For a brief moment, I feel the hairs on the back of my neck rise, the faintest chill brushing over me despite the warmth of the pub. Her fingers linger on mine, cold yet steady, and when she finally pulls back, I feel the absence of her touch like a phantom sensation.

"Shall we?" she asks, her voice light again, as if the weight of her last words had already been forgotten.

I nod, rising to follow her, but the thought remains: What exactly have I just agreed to?

We step outside into the misty gray afternoon, the rain still falling in a soft, steady drizzle. She pops open her umbrella, holding it above us as we walk side by side down the slick cobblestone streets. I feel like I should be the one holding it—but I don't. As we turn a corner, Elise suddenly stops, glancing at her smartwatch with a sharp inhale. Her face tightens, and she mutters under her breath, "Shit."

"What is it?" I ask, startled by her abruptness.

She hesitates, as though caught off guard by her own reaction. "Work," she says finally, her voice clipped. "I completely forgot—I have to go."

"Work? Now?" The words leave my mouth before I can stop them. "On a Sunday?"

She nods, already pulling out her phone and typing something rapidly. "It's a flower shop—Sundays are our busiest day. I didn't realize how late it was." She looks at me then, her expression softening, but there's an edge of urgency she can't quite hide. "I'm sorry. I got caught up… with you."

I try to process her words, the sudden shift in the rhythm of the day. "Can I—should I wait?"

"No." Her response is immediate, almost too quick. "Go back to your hotel, get some rest. I'll call you later, okay?"

Her tone leaves no room for argument, and before I can say more, she leans in, pressing a fleeting kiss to my cheek. "Thank you for today," she whispers. "It meant more than you know."

And just like that, she's gone, her figure disappearing into the rain-slick streets of Whitby. I stand there for a moment, frozen, her kiss still lingering on my skin. The rain soaks through my jacket as the quiet hum of unease settles in my chest.

Whatever just happened, it doesn't feel like the end of a date. It feels like the beginning of a question I don't yet know how to ask.

## CHAPTER 6
# STRAWBERRY WINE

The rain outside my hotel window hadn't stopped since I left Elise in the street. Droplets ran like veins down the glass, tracing paths that seemed aimless and uncertain, much like my thoughts. I'd been sitting on the edge of the stiff bed for hours, staring at my phone. The bright screen mocked me with its stillness: no notifications, no calls, no messages from Elise.

I hated how badly I wanted her to reach out. The connection we had felt real—more than real. It had felt alive, magnetic, undeniable. But now, in the cold quiet of my hotel room, it felt distant. I told myself she'd call. She said she would. Yet with each passing hour, the silence wrapped around me tighter, suffocating and unrelenting.

My phone buzzed suddenly, and my pulse jumped. I snatched it up, hope flaring, only to feel it deflate when I saw the caller ID: "Publisher."

"Alex." My publisher's tone was brisk, impatient. "We need to talk."

I slumped back against the headboard, already knowing

what was coming. "What's up?" I asked, feigning nonchalance, though the tightening in my chest betrayed me.

"What's up?" she repeated, her voice sharp. "What's up is that we're two weeks out from your manuscript deadline, and I still don't have anything from you. Not a draft, not an outline—nothing. Pre-orders are live. Marketing has already started. Do you know how this makes us look?"

I pinched the bridge of my nose, closing my eyes against the dull ache forming there. "I'm working on it," I lied. "It's just… taking longer than I thought."

"That's not going to fly," she snapped. "You signed a contract. You agreed to deliver. Do I need to remind you what's at stake here? Your reputation, your career—"

"I know," I cut her off, my voice sharper than intended. "I know what's at stake."

There was a pause on the other end, heavy with disapproval. "Then act like it," she said finally, her tone ice-cold. "You've got two weeks, Alex. I suggest you use them wisely."

The line went dead before I could respond.

I dropped the phone onto the bed beside me, staring up at the cracked ceiling. Two weeks. Two weeks to deliver something I hadn't even started, something I had no passion for anymore. *Behind the Morning's Glass II*. The sequel no one asked for, the follow-up to the book that had launched my career but left me creatively drained. My publisher didn't care about that, though. To them, I was just a commodity, a name on a cover, a cog in their money-making machine.

And yet, as much as the pressure gnawed at me, it wasn't what occupied my thoughts the most. That space was reserved for her. Elise. Her smile, her laugh, the way her fingers had brushed against mine in the pub. I could still hear her voice, soft and enigmatic: "You're mine."

I reached for my phone again, opening our text thread. It was as barren as the room around me. She hadn't called. She hadn't messaged. But she said she would, right? I typed out a quick message, my thumbs hesitating over the keyboard.

"Hey, hope work isn't too hectic. Miss you already. Call me when you can."

I stared at the words for a long time before hitting send. The message hung there, a tiny blue bubble in a sea of nothingness. I waited, watching the screen as if willing it to light up with a reply. But it didn't. Minutes turned into an hour. Still nothing.

The unease settled deeper in my chest, a hollow ache that refused to be ignored. I couldn't sit here anymore. I needed to get out, to clear my head, to distract myself from the growing void Elise had left in her absence.

Grabbing my coat, I stepped out into the damp evening air. The rain had lessened to a light drizzle, the kind that clung to your skin and made everything feel colder than it was. The streets of Whitby were quiet, the gray light of the moon casting long shadows over everything, particularly the lampposts. Their shadow was long, standing tall against the cobblestones. I wondered if I'd ever feel as confident as their shadows were.

I walked aimlessly at first, letting my feet carry me wherever they wanted. The town felt different now—less charming, more oppressive. Every corner seemed to remind me of her. Eventually, I found myself outside Asda. The fluorescent lights inside spilled out onto the wet pavement, and I ducked in, hoping to find something to take the edge off. The aisles were nearly empty, the shelves sparse, as if the store were winding down for the night. I made my way to the alcohol section, scanning the rows for something strong and cheap.

But the shelves were bare. No whiskey, no beer, not even a dusty bottle of red wine. The only thing left was a small row of strawberry wine, the bottles bright pink and garishly out of place. I stared at them for a long moment, my jaw tightening. "Strawberry wine. I don't want that shit." My eyes darted around; nothing else was there.

"Guess you'll do," I muttered under my breath, grabbing two bottles and heading for the register.

The cashier gave me a bemused look as she scanned the strawberry wine, her eyes lingering on the bottles as if questioning every life decision that had brought me to this point. I didn't bother explaining. What was there to say? That I was buying it to drown my heartbreak over a woman who might not even be thinking about me? That I was unraveling in real time, and this was the best I could do?

"A pack of cigarettes too, please," I added, my voice low.

"Which ones?" she asked, her tone neutral, but her raised eyebrow betrayed a flicker of annoyance.

I pointed toward the first pack I could see. "Benson & Hedges," I said.

She shrugged, reached behind her, and set the pack down on the counter next to the wine. As I stared at the items, a thought struck me, and I glanced at the counter.

"A lighter too, I guess," I said, grabbing a green one from the display and tossing it onto the pile.

She rang it all up, her fingers tapping rhythmically on the register. "Twenty-three quid, fifty," she said.

I handed her a twenty without a word, then fumbled through my pockets for the rest. The coins felt foreign in my hands, the denominations still unfamiliar. Her eyes were on me the entire time, sharp and unrelenting, like she was studying me, peeling back layers. The awkwardness crept up my neck, but I refused to meet her gaze. I'm clearly not from around here.

Finally, I managed to piece together the right amount and slid it across the counter. She counted it methodically, her nails clicking against the coins, then pressed a few buttons on the register.

"Receipt?" she asked flatly.

"No thanks. Cheers," I said, grabbing the bag and stepping back.

"Cheers," she replied, her tone half-hearted, already turning her attention to the guy behind me in line.

I pushed through the double doors of the shop, stepping into the night air. The pavement was still slick and glistening under the fluorescent streetlights of Asda. The bag in my hand felt heavier than it should've, its contents a bitter reminder of the night unraveling in ways I hadn't expected. I didn't bother walking far. Instead, I drifted toward the side of the building, where the light didn't quite reach, and set the bag down on the ground.

I fished out one of the bottles of strawberry wine, twisting off the screw cap with an angry flick of my wrist. The faint hiss of the seal breaking seemed loud in the quiet, and I took a long, burning draw straight from the bottle. It was sickly sweet, artificial, but it went down easier than I'd expected. I wiped my mouth with the back of my hand and slumped against the cold brick wall, letting my weight fall into it.

The pack of cigarettes was next. I tore off the cellophane wrapper and flipped open the top, pulling one out and placing it between my lips. The lighter clicked twice before the flame caught, and I inhaled deeply, feeling the smoke fill my lungs. It wasn't smooth, but it wasn't harsh either—just another distraction, another thing to focus on. I try to ignore things until I forget how I felt in the first place. I tilted my head back and exhaled, watching the smoke curl and dissipate into the night. For a brief moment, the world felt muted, like I was on the outside of it looking in.

The sound of shuffling footsteps snapped me out of my daze. I turned my head to see a man standing a few feet in front of me. He was dressed in a wrinkled gray suit, his hair unkempt and face pale under the harsh glow of the lights. But it wasn't his disheveled appearance that caught my attention—it was the suitcase. A sleek, stainless steel briefcase, handcuffed to his wrist.

"Hey," he said, his voice hoarse, like he hadn't spoken in hours. "You... you know anything about cracking locks?"

I blinked at him, unsure if I'd heard him right. "What?"

"Locks. Suitcases. You know how to get them open?" He stepped closer, his free hand gesturing toward the briefcase as though I hadn't already noticed it.

I took another drag from my cigarette, narrowing my eyes. "No. Why would I?"

He frowned, his gaze darting around nervously before settling back on me. "It's... it's stuck. And I need to get it open. Thought maybe you'd—"

"Look, man," I interrupted, my tone sharp. "I don't know anything about that. Sorry."

But he didn't leave. He lingered there, shifting his weight from foot to foot, the handcuff clinking softly against the handle of the suitcase. "Come on, mate," he said, lowering his voice. "You must know something. Anything. Just... take a look?"

His desperation made me uneasy, and I realized I'd been holding the bottle of strawberry wine in a white-knuckled grip. I set it down at my feet, shaking my head. "I can't help you."

"Please," he said, his voice cracking. "It's important."

The way he said it made my skin crawl. There was something off about him—about this whole situation—and I suddenly felt the overwhelming urge to get out of there. I flicked the cigarette onto the pavement, grinding it out with the toe of my shoe, and stood up straight.

"Sorry," I said again, grabbing the bag and the bottle. "Can't help you."

Before he could say anything else, I turned and started walking, my strides quick and deliberate. I could feel his eyes on me, the weight of his presence lingering like a dart in my back, but I didn't dare turn around. The further I got from the store, the more the tension in my chest eased, though the encounter left a sour taste in my mouth that even the strawberry wine couldn't wash away.

Back in my hotel room, the silence felt heavier than before. I opened the second bottle and took a long swig, the sickly-sweet taste making me wince. It wasn't what I wanted, but it was what I had.

Both bottles went down quicker than I expected. The room spun slightly as I set the second empty bottle down on the nightstand, the clink of glass against wood barely registering. My throat burned, not from the alcohol, but from something else—something deeper. A dry, raw ache that no amount of alcohol could soothe. I leaned back against the headboard, rubbing my neck absentmindedly. The ache there had worsened, spreading from the two faint puncture marks I'd noticed earlier. At first, it had just been a dull throb, but now it felt sharper, like a needle prick that wouldn't go away.

I tilted my head, trying to stretch it out, but the motion

only made me dizzy. My stomach churned uneasily, though I couldn't tell if it was from the wine or something else entirely. I stared at the empty bottles, my reflection warped in their curved surfaces, and tried to make sense of what was happening to me. My body felt foreign, like I was a stranger inhabiting my own skin. I was thirsty, but not for wine. Not for water either. Something else. Something I couldn't name.

I dragged myself off the bed and into the bathroom, the fluorescent light harsh against my eyes. I splashed cold water on my face, hoping it would snap me out of whatever fog I was sinking into. But when I glanced up at the mirror, my breath hitched. The marks on my neck weren't faint anymore. They stood out starkly against my skin, red and angry, as if they'd been made moments ago. I pressed my fingers against them, and a sharp jolt of pain shot through me, forcing me to pull my hand away.

"What the hell is this?" I muttered, staring at my reflection. My face looked pale, almost sallow, like I hadn't slept in days. My eyes were bloodshot, the veins in them spidering out in a way that made me flinch. I stumbled back from the sink, gripping the edges of the counter for dear life as a wave of dizziness overtook me. My breathing quickened, shallow and erratic, as I tried to steady myself. I glanced up again, desperate to make sense of what I was seeing—or rather, what I wasn't seeing.

My reflection was gone.

At first, I thought it was the light, maybe the harsh fluorescents casting some strange shadow or distortion. But no matter how I turned my head or moved, the mirror didn't show me. It reflected the bathroom behind me—the tiles, the towel hanging on the rack, the bottle of hotel soap on the counter—but not me. Not my face, not my body. Nothing.

I reached out hesitantly, my fingers brushing against the cool glass. The surface was smooth, solid, exactly what it should be. And yet, I wasn't there. My chest tightened as I stared at the empty space where I should have been, my mind scrambling for answers. Was I hallucinating? How drunk am I exactly, what's happening? My throat clenched, dry and aching, as panic began to creep in.

"No," I whispered to myself, shaking my head. "This isn't real. This isn't happening."

I waved my hand in front of the mirror, watching as the air moved but the glass remained empty. It was impossible, surreal, like stepping into a nightmare I couldn't wake from. My fingers went to my neck again, tracing the outline of the puncture marks. They were hot to the touch, pulsing faintly beneath my skin, as if they had a life of their own.

I turned away from the mirror, unable to look at the void any longer. My stomach churned, a hollow ache spreading through my chest. I stumbled back into the main room, the dim light from the bedside lamp casting long figments on the walls. My throat burned worse than ever, and my tongue felt like sandpaper in my mouth. I grabbed the half-empty bottle of water I'd left on the nightstand and took a swig, only to spit it out immediately. The taste was metallic, bitter, like I'd just drunk something spoiled.

My legs buckled, and I sank onto the edge of the bed, my hands gripping the sheets tightly. The thirst was unbearable now, clawing at me from the inside out. It wasn't just physical—it was something deeper, something primal. My head throbbed, my pulse hammering in my ears as I tried to make sense of what was happening to me.

I looked down at my hands, my fingers trembling

uncontrollably. They looked paler than usual, the veins beneath the skin more pronounced, almost like they were glowing faintly blue under the dim light. My breath hitched as the realization began to settle in: whatever was happening, it wasn't normal. It wasn't something I could explain away with logic or reason.

I stood abruptly, the motion making me stagger slightly. My gaze darted to the window, the pale glow of the moon casting a faint light into the room. I felt drawn to it, inexplicably, like it was calling to me. My steps were unsteady as I approached the window, pressing my forehead against the cold glass. The world outside felt distant, like I was watching it through a screen. The thirst clawed at me again, sharper this time, and I bit down on my lip to keep from crying out.

What was happening to me? The thought repeated in my mind, relentless, as I stood there, trembling and hollow. I closed my eyes, trying to will the sensations away, but they only grew stronger. The hunger. The thirst. The ache in my neck. The emptiness where my reflection should have been.

I opened my eyes and turned back toward the room, the emptiness inside me threatening to consume everything. I reached for my phone on the nightstand, my fingers fumbling as I unlocked it. Elise. I needed to call her, to hear her voice. My fingers hovered over her name, but I hesitated. Would she even pick up? Would she even care?

The screen blurred as my eyes filled with tears, and I dropped the phone onto the bed, my shoulders sagging under the weight of everything I couldn't explain. My gaze drifted back to the empty wine bottles, their bright pink labels mocking me from the nightstand.

The thirst wouldn't go away. It wouldn't stop. It was

consuming me, gnawing at my sanity, and I didn't know how much longer I could hold on.

At some point, I must have fallen asleep—or passed out. When I woke, the room was still dark, the only light coming from the faint glow of the moon outside. The hunger was still there, but it felt different now. Quieter. More controlled. But the thirst? That hadn't changed. If anything, it was worse.

I stood slowly, my body weak and unsteady, and made my way to the window. The cool air hit my face, and for a moment, I felt almost normal. Almost. But deep down, I knew nothing was normal anymore. I wasn't the same person I'd been yesterday. Something was happening to me, something I didn't understand. And the worst part? I wasn't sure I wanted to.

"She's not going to call," I said aloud, my voice bitter and slurred. "You're an idiot for thinking she would."

The words hung in the air, stark and unforgiving. I took the last swig of the water at my bedside, draining the last of it before tossing the bottle onto the floor. It rolled under the bed with a hollow, empty clink.

"She played you," I muttered, my voice barely above a whisper. "Gaslit you. Made you think you were special."

I grabbed my phone, unlocking it to check for messages. Still nothing. The blue bubble from earlier stared back at me, its silence louder than any reply could have been.

"Fuck," I muttered, dropping the phone onto the bed. The ache in my chest had spread, twisting into something darker, something I couldn't shake. It wasn't just about Elise anymore. It was everything—the deadline I couldn't meet, the book I didn't want to write, the life I felt slipping through my fingers. I wanted to go away—to get as far as I could from these thoughts, these feelings that clawed their way into me. But she was still there, in the back of my mind, her voice reverberating: "You're mine."

"Bullshit," I said aloud, my voice cracking. "I'm no one's."

The room spun as I stood, sanity slipping from my mind and shattering on the floor. I collapsed onto the bed, the weight of the day finally pulling me under.

## CHAPTER 7
# GLUE MYSELF SHUT

The knock at the door was sharp—too sharp. It cleaved through the darkness of my hotel room like an axe, and for a moment I wasn't sure if I'd dreamed it. My mouth was dry, my head pounding with a low, throbbing ache that seemed to come from somewhere deeper than the skull.

Another knock. Louder this time.

I sat up slowly, every bone creaking, every joint stiff. The room spun slightly before it steadied. It was dark out. Hadn't it been morning? Or afternoon? I reached for my phone. The screen glared back at me—10:17 p.m. Notifications flooded the lock screen like a tidal wave. Thirty missed calls. Dozens of messages.

All from Elise.

The knock came again.

I hesitated. My heart picked up its pace, thudding uncomfortably in my chest. I stood, bare feet cold against the worn carpet, and shuffled toward the door. My voice cracked when I spoke.

"I'm not… feeling great," I said, loud enough for

whoever was on the other side to hear. "Maybe come back tomorrow?"

"Elise," she said, unmistakably.

I froze. I'd imagined her voice all day—soft, coiling through my memory like a thread I couldn't pull free. But this wasn't memory. She was here.

"Elise?"

"You didn't answer your phone," she said, her voice muffled slightly by the door. "You weren't at the pub. I got worried."

I fumbled with the latch and cracked the door, keeping the chain lock in place. Her face appeared in the gap, framed by the corridor's yellow glow.

"I said I'm not feeling well," I repeated. "I—"

She pushed.

The chain held for a breath, maybe two, then snapped with a metallic clink. The door flew open and I stumbled back, nearly tripping over my own feet.

"Elise—what the hell—"

But she didn't look angry. Just determined. Concerned, even. She stepped inside and closed the door gently behind her.

"You look terrible," she said, smiling while scanning me from head to toe. She walked past me like she'd been here before and sat down on the edge of my bed.

I stared, still not sure if I was awake.

"I tried to call," she said, brushing her hair from her face. "Texted you. Dozens of times."

"I just saw," I said, holding up my phone. "I guess I slept through the day."

"Clearly."

Her eyes narrowed. "What are your symptoms?"

"Symptoms?" I asked, blinking.

"Yes," she said calmly. "Tell me everything."

"I don't know," I said, rubbing my neck. "My throat's dry. Really dry. I drank water, but it tasted... off. Like metal."

She nodded. "What else?"

"I ache. Everywhere. My head's pounding. My skin feels weird. Cold one second, burning the next. I feel... wrong. Like my body isn't mine anymore."

She studied me with unnerving focus.

"Do your eyes hurt?" she asked.

I hesitated. "Only in the light. The bathroom lights made me dizzy."

"And the mirror?"

I looked at her, startled. "What about it?"

"Could you see yourself?"

I didn't answer.

"Elise," I said slowly. "What's happening to me?"

She didn't flinch. "Anything else?"

"My appetite's gone," I said. "But I'm starving. And thirsty. And nothing helps. Not wine. Not water. It's like I'm dying of something I can't describe."

Her gaze was steady. "You're not dying."

"Then what am I?"

She stood up and walked toward me, close enough that I could feel her breath, hear her heartbeat—the smell something faintly floral and coppery beneath her perfume. My senses were in overdrive.

"Are you hungry now?" she asked.

I hesitated. "Yeah."

"But for what?" she asked gently.

Her voice didn't sound like an accusation. It was like she already knew the answer and was just waiting for me to say it.

"I don't know," I murmured. "Something. I don't know what."

She looked into my eyes like she was searching for something. Then she nodded, once, like she'd found it.

"We need to talk," she said. "I have a bit of a confession to make."

I sank into the chair near the window, feeling the weight of everything I couldn't name press down on me.

"Elise," I said again, quieter this time. "What did you do to me?"

She didn't answer. Just stood there, watching me unravel, as if the truth were something I had to bleed out on my own.

I rubbed my hands over my face. "You're not going to say anything?"

"I'm deciding where to start."

Her voice was gentle. Too gentle. It scared me more than if she'd screamed.

I followed her gaze as it flicked to the desk in the corner of the room. A letter opener rested on its edge—brass-handled, narrow, gleaming faintly under the lamp. I don't remember putting it there. I don't remember ever using it.

She walked over to it without a word, lifted it, and turned back to face me.

"Elise." I stood. "What the hell are you doing?"

She didn't answer. Just looked at me for a long time—long enough that I almost said her name again.

Then she dragged the blade across her forearm in one clean stroke.

I flinched. "Jesus Christ—"

But there was no panic in her face. No pain. Just a slow blink, like she'd done something as mundane as opening a bottle of wine. The skin parted like silk, and blood welled up instantly—thicker than I expected. Darker. It didn't fall. It shimmered. Almost... pulsed.

I couldn't move.

"Elise," I said again, but my voice was gone. Hollow. Empty.

She crossed the space between us and held out her arm.

"Drink," she said, like it was nothing.

I shook my head. "You're insane."

"You're starving."

"I'm not—"

But I was. The smell hit me first—metallic, sweet, alive. My stomach twisted, and I staggered back a step. My throat burned. Not like thirst. Not like anything I'd ever felt before. It was heat, it was pressure, it was need. I wanted to vomit. I wanted to scream. I wanted to lunge.

"Elise—what the fuck did you do to me—"

"Drink," she said again, and this time it wasn't a request. It was gravity.

I didn't remember moving. One breath I was upright, resisting. The next I was on my knees, her wrist pressed against my mouth.

I didn't taste it. I felt it.

It was everything. Fire and velvet—air and truth. It filled the hollowed-out parts of me like molten silver. I drank and drank and felt the world fold inward—my pain dulling, the ache in my neck disappearing, the fever burning off like mist.

When she pulled her arm away, I gasped like I'd been underwater. My mouth was stained red. I wiped it with the back of my hand, ashamed, afraid, electrified.

I stared at her like she was a God that had just torn open the sky.

"You're not lying," I said, my voice rough.

"No."
"This is real."
"Yes."
"You turned me."
She nodded.

I sat back, spine hitting the dresser. "Say it. Say what you are."

She crouched to meet me at eye level.

"I'm a vampire," she said. "At least that's what they call us."

I let the words hang there. They sounded ridiculous, even now. And yet every cell in my body screamed otherwise. My reflection gone. My skin. The ache. The thirst. The way her blood made everything stop hurting.

"I should hate you," I proclaimed.

"You don't."

I didn't answer.

She sat beside me, legs folded underneath her, arm already healing before my eyes. No scar. No evidence.

"It's not what you think," she said. "It's not mythology. It's genetic. A mutation. We call it Morbus Sanguiatis. An old name. It's passed on through blood. And only if you survive the bite."

"So this is... a disease?"

"A very old one. One that's not supposed to exist. But it does. And now it's in you."

I ran my hand over my head, pacing the edges of my own unraveling. "So what now? I go drink from people? Bite strangers in alleyways? You teach me how to turn into a bat?"

"This isn't a movie, Alex."

"You don't say."

"There are rules," she said, her tone soft but firm. "Limits. Risks."

I looked at her, the nausea crawling back in. "Do I have to kill?"

"Does anyone?" she said immediately. "You don't have to kill. You just have to feed."

"And if I don't?"

"You'll die."

I laughed, short and dry and bitter. "Of course."

"You asked what you are," she said, standing again, walking toward the window. "You're not undead. You're not cursed. You're changed. Evolved, in a way. But this gene—it doesn't ask politely. It takes what it wants."

I sat down hard on the edge of the bed.

"Why me?" I asked.

"Alex," she said, softly, but without apology. "When we met in the pub… you said you were looking for me."

I blinked.

"And at the Abbey…" She drew in closer, her voice steady. "You told me you were mine."

I remembered.

"You gave yourself to me long before I ever touched you. I didn't steal anything."

She sat back, watching me.

"I only gave you what you asked for. We have to be invited in—and you invited me, Alex."

I didn't answer. Couldn't. She didn't press me.

Instead, Elise leaned back against the window ledge, silhouetted in the weak amber light that bled in from the streetlamp outside. Her outline was still—too still. Like a photograph of motion that had been paused just before something irreversible.

"How long do I have?" I asked, finally.

"To what?" Her voice was velvet and restraint.

"Until I lose myself."

She tilted her head slightly. "You won't. Not if you understand what this is."

"You called it a mutation."

She nodded. "Morbus Sanguiatis. It's older than language. But yes, that's what it is. A rare gene mutation, an autoimmune disease passed through blood. It rewrites your biology. Slowly at first. Then all at once. Not everyone can live through it."

I swallowed, my mouth still tasting of blood and shame. "So you could have killed me?"

"It was a possibility, yes. But I could tell, through your smell, your kiss—when we made love," she said. "I knew you would survive it, I sensed it. We have a seventh sense —if you will. Everything is heightened, taste, smell, cognitive ability, intuition... everything. I know what you're thinking now, for example—no, you're not cursed. You're not damned. You're just a new version of you—a better version, mutated. You just have to be careful with some things."

"How careful?"

"Careful enough to stay out of sunlight. Careful enough to feed before the thirst turns you feral. Careful enough to know when to run, and when to stop pretending you're still like them."

Them. That word held more weight than I was ready for.

I looked up. "Tell me everything. I want to know. I want all of it."

Elise folded her arms across her chest, watching me for a long beat before answering.

"We're not cold because we're dead," she said. "Our

hearts still beat. Just slowly—ten times a minute, give or take."

I blinked. "That's not possible."

"It is. Barely. It keeps us alive, just enough. But it's also why we feel distant. Cold to the touch. Why our blood moves like honey and our warmth never quite returns."

"Is that why you live so long?"

She nodded once. "The slow heart preserves the body. Metabolism is slowed and optimized, cells regenerate, but they don't decay the way they used to. Most of us stop aging entirely around thirty."

"And if your heart stops?"

Her eyes met mine. "We die. Just like anyone else. The difference is how hard it is to kill us. And how easy it is... if you know where to strike."

I exhaled. "A stake through the heart?"

"Not wood. That's a myth. It just has to pierce the heart completely and remain in our heart for too long. We can survive most wounds—but the heart is fragile. Slower to heal. If you puncture and leave something protruding in it, the muscle fails. It can't restart. It can't correctly regenerate. You'll bleed out internally before the gene can repair the damage."

I let the silence settle, uneasy in my skin. "And decapitation?"

"That one's true," she said flatly. "The body can't regenerate what it doesn't have."

I flinched.

"Who the hell figured all this out?"

She gave me a wry, tired smile. "Trial and error. A lot of it."

"And the sun?" I asked. "What happens if I step outside?"

Her gaze darkened.

"You'll feel it immediately," she said. "Not like a sunburn burn. Like an acid burn. The gene interferes with melanin—blocks it entirely. So your skin doesn't protect you at all from the sun. A few minutes in direct sunlight and you're blistering like you were cooked alive. A few more and your skin will start to slough off entirely."

I looked away, jaw tightening.

"It's not fire," she added. "It doesn't make you explode. It just cooks you alive."

"Jesus."

"You'll learn to feel it," she said. "Even behind glass, you'll flinch. Like your body remembers what it can't handle anymore."

I rubbed my hands together, trying to make the chill leave me. It didn't.

"What about garlic?" I asked, half-joking.

"Anaphylaxis," she said, not smiling. "Any plant in the allium family. Garlic, leeks, chives, shallots. The gene reacts violently. Our airways close, organs seize. It's fatal if you don't get treatment in time. An EpiPen works just fine. You should carry one—just in case."

I swallowed hard. "So every myth is just a bad translation."

"They always are."

"And mirrors?"

She hesitated.

"That one's... complicated," she said. "We do cast reflections. But only sometimes. It's about light—about how our skin reflects it. The way it bends. We metabolize differently. Cameras struggle too—older lenses, especially. You'll see yourself blurred, smeared. Like the light doesn't want to touch you."

I looked toward the bathroom door. The mirror inside. The one I hadn't dared return to since the afternoon.

"Why now?" I asked. "Why me?"

Elise didn't answer right away. She moved from the window and crossed the room again, her steps silent on the threadbare carpet. She crouched beside me like she had before, and for the first time, I noticed how still she was—no idle fidgeting, no unconscious shifts. Just the low hum of something ancient, watching.

"You were already unraveling," she said softly. "Already searching. All I did was... needle the thread."

I looked at her. Really looked.

"And now what?"

"Now you choose."

She stood and offered her hand.

"You can fight it. Starve. Fade. Die. Try to pretend none of this happened. Or you can learn. Adapt. Let go of who you thought you were."

I didn't move.

"You said you were mine," she reminded me.

"I did."

"Then come," she said, her voice like night. "I'll teach you how to survive."

I took her hand. It was cold. But mine was colder.

## CHAPTER 8
# THE AURA OF HUNGER

The pubs hadn't emptied, not entirely. Laughter still crawled up from the harbor-side, low and loose with alcohol. But the further we walked from the lights, the more the night changed—sharpened. Whitby doesn't sleep, not really. It waits. Fog slipped between buildings like it was listening for something.

Elise didn't tell me where we were going. Only that I needed to see. Needed to learn. The hunt, she said, is not about violence. It's about clarity. There are rules to it. You have to know what to look for.

"You're not a monster," she said, as we stepped beyond the last row of houses, the street-lamps flickering behind us. "But you're not what you were either. That part of you's gone. What you are now needs truth to survive. And truth doesn't hide."

We crossed the river via the Swing Bridge, its wooden planks slick underfoot. Whitby looked different from the east bank—quieter, smaller, half-swallowed by its own mystery. She led me through backstreets I hadn't seen before, alleys that bled into gravel paths, the sound of our footsteps muffled beneath the weight of the mist.

I didn't ask questions. I just followed.

I felt... tuned. Like my ears could hear past walls. Like my eyes were adjusting to some light no one else could see. And I could feel them—people. Not near, but pulsing on the edge of perception. Their emotions. Their heat. Their very essence. It was as if the world had thinned, the veil peeled back, and everything underneath was raw and obvious.

But I wasn't prepared for the color.

"The aura comes after," Elise said. "It's not literal light. It's a signature. A presence. Their nervous system leaves a trail in the air. It's not visible. Not quite. But you'll know."

We turned down a slope near Spital Bridge, where the edge of Fishburn Park met the industrial sprawl. The area was grimed with decades of failure—warehouses, forgotten lots, a burned-out mechanic shop. The only light was a half-dead security lamp flickering above a rusted fence.

"This is where they come," she said. "Men who think no one sees them. Men who take what they want and disappear before morning. Women too, sometimes. But mostly men."

I said nothing. But I felt it.

The wrongness.

A pressure behind my eyes, like walking into a room still filled with the remnants of a scream reverberating off the walls. My skin bristled. My stomach coiled. My hunger sharpened.

"Elise," I said quietly. "Someone's here."

She nodded. "Good."

And then I saw him.

At the far end of the alley, near a dumpster, half-hidden by the dark. A man hunched over something—or someone

—I couldn't tell. But I didn't need to. My blood knew before I did.

He glowed.

Not brightly. Not fully. But with a stain. A halo of violent memory. It wasn't visible in the way sunlight is, but it was there. Like a scent you can taste. Purple. Dark purple. Like bruised grapes, like clotted wine.

My breath caught.

"That's the color of death," she explained. "Not their death. Someone else's. You're not seeing guilt. You're seeing the residue of blood spilled by their hand. And not in defense. Not by accident. Real death. That stain never fades."

"He's—"

"A killer," she said. "A recent one. Maybe his first. Maybe not."

I stepped forward, barely aware of my own feet.

"Elise. What do we do?"

She placed a hand on my chest. Stopped me.

"I do. You watch."

The air shifted.

She moved with stillness first—unnerving calm. Not predatory, not theatrical. Just precise. No wasted breath. No wasted step.

He didn't even look up until she was near. He turned, startled, mouth opening to speak. And then she had him—gently, terribly. One hand behind his head, the other around his jaw, as if helping him drink from a glass. He never screamed. She didn't let him.

I saw the blood before I smelled it. Thick. Slow. Alive. Her mouth moved against his throat like a kiss that knew too much. His aura flared—one last burst of purple, then it died. Extinguished. Like it had never been there at all.

She looked up.

Her lips were wet. Her eyes glowing faintly from within. She said nothing. Just tilted her wrist. A silent offering.

I stepped forward, half-dreaming.

I thought I'd be sick. That the shame would hit me before the desire. That I'd feel like I was stealing something sacred.

But I was starving.

"Drink from me first," she said. "It eases the transition. You haven't had human blood yet—not really. Not alone."

I drank.

Not from the throat, but from her wrist—her blood, already warmed with his. I felt it. Entering me like heat breaking ice. The static in my mind cleared. The ache in my bones evaporated. The hunger didn't vanish—it opened.

Behind it came clarity.

I saw it all.

The man on the ground—what he'd done. Not in pictures. In sensation. The fear he caused. The false power he wielded. The emptiness inside him that sought something to hurt.

I pulled away, gasping.

Elise wiped her wrist on her sleeve, the wound already gone. She stared at the man's body. Not with regret. Not even satisfaction.

Just silence.

I dropped to my knees.

"You knew," I said. "You knew what he was."

She nodded.

"I can't kill people," I whispered. "I'm not—"

"You didn't," she said. "I did. You fed. That's what you needed to understand. We don't hunt the innocent. We don't feed from the clean. You'll see. You'll feel it. Their aura tells you who they are."

I looked down at the body.

"It's like I know all of him—all of his sin. I feel it."

She crouched beside me.

"You always will," she said. "That's the tax. We carry the ones we feed on. We inherit their pain, their blood, their memory. If it was easy, it wouldn't be ethical."

I shook.

She reached for my hand.

"You said you wanted to understand. Now you do. The hunger is part of you now. But you decide who feeds it."

I looked at her.

And for the first time, I saw it too.

No aura. No glow. No color.

Just absence. Just silence. Just her.

We stood.

The man's body was already cooling. His story, for now, ended. My own, just beginning.

I stared at him—at the slackness in his jaw, the blood on his collar, the strange peace in death I hadn't expected to see. There was no ceremony. No thunder. Just stillness. And hunger, receding.

Elise didn't move. She didn't need to. The silence between us said everything.

"He was ready," she said finally. "Some part of him knew what was coming. Some part always does."

I looked away, trying not to let the tremor in my hands return. "I thought I'd feel guilt."

"Do you?"

I opened my mouth, but there was no answer waiting.

We walked. Away from the body. Away from the light. Deeper into the folds of Whitby where the cobblestones split and buildings leaned like old men trading secrets. The air smelled of salt and fog and something iron-sweet that clung to my senses like a film.

"Tell me about the auras again," I said. "I need to understand."

She glanced at me sideways. Her expression unreadable. "It's not magic, Alex. It's sensory. Advanced pattern recognition. But that doesn't make it any less real."

"Then what is it?"

"It's instinct. Refined. The gene changes us in layers. Some chemical. Some cognitive. We see things we didn't before. Patterns of harm. Of violence. Blood doesn't forget—it leaves traces. In their eyes. In the pitch of their voice. In their scent. We perceive it as color, but it's more like... presence. A kind of psychic resonance."

I nodded slowly, absorbing it like scripture. "And the colors?"

"White," she said, "is the untouched. People who've never killed, never crossed that threshold. Red means harm. Intent. A soul unraveling in real time. But purple... purple means they've done it. Taken life. Cold or not. They carry it in them."

"And us?"

She looked ahead. "We don't cast. Not anymore. We're the absence. A void surrounded by light."

We passed under a crooked archway that led into what looked like the remnants of an old market lane. Graffiti scratched against stone. A broken bottle glinted beneath a flickering gas-lamp. The fog had thickened now, like it was hiding something.

"There," Elise said.

I saw him before I felt it—though the feeling came next, sudden and nauseating. Like a cold nail driven into the back of my skull. He was slouched near the end of the alley, lighting a cigarette with one hand, scrolling on his phone with the other. The glow lit his face enough to see the hollowness in it.

"Purple," I said.

"Deep," she said. "Darker than the last."

My stomach twisted. "What did he do?"

She shook her head. "Don't ask. Doesn't matter. Not tonight."

"I need to know—"

"No, Alex." Her voice was a hush but a command. "Don't think. Don't analyze. Don't make it moral. Let your instincts in. That's the only way you survive."

I stood frozen, heart hammering. The ache had returned, low and slow, like a tide rising in my spine.

"But what if I'm wrong?" I asked.

"You're not. You see it just as I do," she said. "Auras don't lie—they can't. The body knows. The blood knows."

I turned back toward the man. His aura had changed now that I knew how to see it. Like watching a bruise spread beneath skin. The color wasn't metaphor. It was presence. It throbbed. It pulsed.

I stepped toward him.

My breath shallowed. My jaw clenched. My bones thrummed with something not entirely mine. There was no thought. Only movement. One foot. Then the next.

And still she said nothing.

This was mine.

My first.

The man didn't look up—not right away. Just kept thumbing his screen, dragging long on his cigarette like the night owed him quiet. I could hear the blood in his throat, feel the beat of it like a low drum inside my own ears. Close now. Close enough to smell the whiskey coming through his pores. He was drunk.

Then he looked up.

His eyes flicked to mine, blank for a second—then narrowed. His lips parted, cigarette hanging loose, and I saw it. Recognition. Not of me. Of something older. Primal. He smelled it on me the way prey knows it's already bleeding.

"What the fuck do you want?" he snapped, standing, straightening, shoulders stiff.

I said nothing. I didn't need to. The hunger had taken hold—total, consuming. But not mindless. Focused.

I lunged.

It wasn't graceful. Nothing like Elise—no blur, no predator's elegance. I hit him hard, shoulder into chest, and we both slammed into the alley wall. His head cracked the brick. He yelled, elbowed back, and we grappled, slipping over trash and broken glass. I was stronger—I could feel it—but not coordinated. Not yet. I hadn't learned my body. I hadn't earned it.

He recovered first.

A flick of movement—steel glinting.

The blade entered me just below the ribs. I gasped, the breath stolen from my lungs like a vacuum. The pain wasn't sharp—it was deep, spreading outward in wet heat. He shoved me off, and I stumbled, hit the wall, and slid down.

Everything spun.

The man's breathing was fast now, panicked. He looked down at the blood on his knife, then at me, like he couldn't believe I was still conscious. I shouldn't have been.

"You crazy bastard," he muttered. "What the fuck are you?"

I looked down. Blood. My blood. But it wasn't like

before. It was slower, thicker—already clotting at the edges. I could feel it trying to stitch me shut. Trying to save me. But not fast enough.

I tried to stand.

He kicked me.

Hard. I felt the edge of his boot across my face as my vision slipped into stars.

My head slammed the brick behind me, and for a second the world was just white light and pressure. My hands scrabbled at the ground, at his boots, trying to find leverage, anything, but I was too slow.

He raised the knife again.

And then Elise was there.

No sound. No warning.

One second it was him. The next—it wasn't.

She moved like the devil himself, like a silent storm. One hand on his throat. The other on his wrist. The knife clattered to the ground before he knew it was gone. He gurgled, feet kicking at nothing, clawing at her arm as she lifted him, spine arched, back against the alley wall.

"Enough," she said, calm as rain.

He tried to scream.

She sank her teeth into his throat before he could.

It wasn't gentle.

She ripped through the flesh like silk gone taut. The sound was soft, wet, final. Blood cascaded out in all directions like an explosion. It painted my face in speckles. It spilled down his chest, staining him in red as his arms jerked once, twice, then fell limp. His head lolled. The color left him in seconds.

When she let go, he dropped like meat hitting concrete. I'll never forget that sound.

Elise turned to me, blood covering her entire face, chest rising and falling with restraint.

"You hesitated," she said.

I winced, trying to sit up. "I didn't think he'd fight like that."

"They always fight," she said, kneeling beside me. "That's what makes them dangerous. That's what makes them worth it."

I looked down at the wound. It still bled, but the pain was dulling. The skin already puckering at the edges. "He stabbed me."

"Yes," she said. "And next time, he'll do worse—unless you stop flinching. You can't hesitate. You need to be fast, violent. They can't have a chance to react."

I looked at her, shame pooling somewhere behind my ribs.

"You didn't fail," she added, softer now. "You learned."

Then she leaned in and held her wrist to my mouth again.

"Drink," she said. "Heal."

I hesitated—barely—but the instinct was louder than guilt. Her skin split open like it had been waiting, and I pressed my mouth to the wound. Her blood didn't rush. It poured slow, deliberate, like honey through a pinprick.

I drank.

It wasn't like before.

This time it didn't burn.

It floated.

My limbs turned warm, almost weightless. The shame blurred, softened. My thoughts slowed, just enough to lose their edges. I blinked hard.

"Elise..." I murmured. "I feel... drunk."

She smiled faintly, like that had been the point.

"You are," she said. "He was."

She continued, brushing her hair back from her forehead. "It lingers in the blood. Anything in the bloodstream does. Alcohol. Opiates. Adrenaline. Don't worry about it. You will be sober soon enough."

"We need to clean up before we get back to town. Follow me."

# CHAPTER 9
# A WAKING KIND OF TRUTH

When I woke up, she was already watching me.

I didn't startle. I just opened my eyes to her gaze, steady and close. Her bare shoulder pressed against mine, her knees drawn up beneath the sheets like she'd never moved. Maybe she hadn't. Maybe she didn't have to.

"Do you always watch people sleep?" I asked.

She tilted her head slightly, but didn't smile. "Only you."

The silence between us wasn't empty. It pulsed. The room was dim, lit only by what little dusk bled through the edges of blackout curtains. The air tasted faintly of copper and breath and something warmer. Familiar. My body ached, but not from injury. From release.

I didn't remember falling asleep. Only her hands. Her mouth. The feeling of being undone and then remade.

Elise traced the edge of my jaw with her knuckle. "You were still healing. Sleep helps."

"And the rest?"

She didn't answer, not with words. She leaned in, slow, pressing her mouth to mine. Not hungry. Not sweet. Just sure. It didn't matter how new I was to this life—I knew she could feel it. How quickly I responded. How easily I gave myself over.

I pulled her on top of me. She didn't resist.

We moved like we had the first time—wordless, instinctive, unhurried. But there was something different now. Something darker threading between our bodies. Something deeper. A mutual erosion. Something inevitable.

Watching her on top of me, feeling her nails dig into my chest—it wasn't just sex.

It was surrender.

She moved like she was unmaking me, and I let her. Every breath, every press of her hips was a command I didn't question. My hands gripped her waist, then her shoulders, then her face—like I couldn't decide if I wanted to hold her or fall apart beneath her.

Her hair fell over me like a curtain, her lips brushing mine between gasps, between silences that said more than speech could hold. I tasted blood once. I wasn't sure if it was hers or mine. I didn't care.

Her name left my mouth in pieces. Not a word, a need.

The way she closed her eyes, before staring straight through mine. It wasn't just full of lust, it felt full of sin—and it was delicious. Forbidden, unraveling pleasure. She moaned louder, teeth bared. I bit my lip to stay quiet. She didn't let me. She leaned in, licking my blood before allowing her lips to find mine. She buried herself further, I could feel myself getting deeper and deeper inside of her.

"Elise..." I moaned. Both of our breathing rhythmically increased. Our hearts beat in lockstep. She grasped me tighter, went harder. What felt like an hour erupted into one final moan as her thighs gripped me tighter. I pulled her in closer, embracing the throbbing of her orgasm. Feeling her nails release from my chest as she finished.

With her mouth grazing my ear, she gently bit me. "You're mine," she said, but softer now. Not as a threat. As a truth I'd already accepted.

I reached up, dragged my fingers down her back, memorizing the shape of her spine, the way her body shivered when I touched the small of it. She kissed me then—not gently. It was bruising. Desperate. Like she didn't want me, she needed me.

And I realized—so did I.

It wasn't possession. It was fusion. Like something in me had always been shaped to fit her.

When I came apart, it wasn't release. It was ruin.

And she watched me unravel like she'd known it would happen all along.

Like she'd been waiting for it.

I didn't say I love you.

She knew I didn't have to.

She owned me; my existence was on lease to her.

After, she lay against my chest, breathing steady. I traced the ridges of her spine, one by one.

"Are you mine?" I asked.

She laughed once. Quiet. Cruel. "That's not how it works."

"But I'm yours."

"Yes."

She didn't say it as a confession. She said it like fact. Like gravity. I didn't resent it.

I let the silence sit for a while, trying to make sense of

the stillness in my limbs. There was a heaviness that wasn't exhaustion. Not fully. I blinked up at the ceiling.

"What are we then?"

She kissed me. "Whatever I tell you we are."

I didn't know how to respond—I knew she was right.

"Is that a problem?"

"I—don't know."

She put both of her hands on my face. "Don't worry—you will figure it out."

"I will figure what out?"

She smiled. "Don't ask questions that you already know the answer to."

I laid with her in silence. In fear, but also in a muddied confusion of emotions. I knew exactly what she meant. I was afraid to admit it.

I deflected after a few moments, "What time is it?"

She didn't move. "Almost eight."

"Morning?"

"Evening."

I looked to my watch, confirming. It had blood on it from last night.

"You should clean that off," she said, noticing it the same time as me.

She continued, "You know, time really isn't important anymore. You really don't need that relic anymore."

"Relic? Exactly how old are you?"

She slapped me playfully, but it still hurt. "It's not polite to ask a lady her age."

I exhaled. "So that's it. Night is our morning now."

"It doesn't have to be," she said. "But it's easier. Safer."

I sat up slowly, the sheet falling from my chest. I checked my torso for a knife wound. Nothing, not even a scar.

Her flat was small, sparse, clean. One bookshelf. No television. No photos. Nothing to indicate a past. Just clothes folded neatly on a chair and an empty glass on the windowsill.

"You don't have much," I said.

"I don't keep much."

"Why?"

She turned her face toward me, the dim light catching in her eyes like reflection off water. "Because nothing lasts. Not really. You live long enough, you learn not to tether yourself to anything that can be taken."

She sat up then, reaching for the robe on the floor. As she moved, I noticed something strange—no scars. Not a single one. Her skin, dark and flawless and unmarred, looked almost unreal.

"So we heal from anything?"

"Almost anything. I already told you that."

"I know—it's just hard to believe."

She nodded. "Well, believe this: we're not immortal, Alex. Just... re-written."

I stood, stretching, trying to reacquaint myself with my own body. There was no stiffness. No soreness. Just a low, humming charge beneath the skin.

"Do we eat?" I asked. "Drink?"

She shrugged. "We can. We don't need to. But sometimes... it helps to blend in. Sit in a pub, have a pint. Makes the world feel normal. Makes us feel less apart from it."

I glanced toward the covered window, out of habit I guess. The curtain was shut tight, but a sliver of dying sunlight peeked through. I felt nothing looking at it. No fear. Just a vague, animal sense of avoidance.

Elise stood by the window, pulling the curtain back just an inch. She didn't look at me when she spoke next.

"You'll need to feed again soon. We're going out tonight, I want you to meet the others."

I didn't ask who the others were. I didn't have to. The tone in her voice sharpened something primal in my chest —anticipation, maybe, or something that resembled loyalty. As she showered, I didn't know if I should run. I didn't know if this was a dream or a nightmare but in some grotesque way—I knew that I didn't want to wake up.

Elise dressed in silence, all unhurried movements and effortless elegance. I moved slower, still caught in the weight of what she'd said. We're not immortal. Just re-written. I could feel it. In my bones. In the way my senses hadn't dulled after climax—they'd sharpened.

The Black Horse Inn wasn't far. A ten-minute walk, maybe less. But the world felt different now, like I was seeing it through wet glass. Every lamp flicker along the cobblestones pulsed too bright. Every voice in the distance carried too far. My body adjusted as we walked, syncing to something deeper than breath. Something ancestral. Animal.

Whitby was alive at night in the way the day could never manage. The sea groaned somewhere beyond the town's narrow streets. The old stones bled salt and forgotten footsteps. And above it all, the Abbey loomed like a wound on the sky. Waiting.

Elise reached for my hand without looking, lacing her fingers through mine like it belonged to her. Maybe it did. Maybe I didn't care.

The Black Horse was dimly lit—dark wood beams, low laughter, the faint smell of damp earth and something roasted.

Now I could hear it—the difference. I could hear every

voice individually, not as a roar of collective chatter. It was overwhelming.

There was a rhythm beneath the noise, a kind of internal percussion to the conversations happening inside. A heartbeat that didn't match mine. A pulse out of time.

"They're already here," Elise said.

It was difficult seeing past the faint glow of everyone's auras. Until I saw four individuals in the back without any aura at all. I knew instantly, that's them.

The booth was in the farthest corner. Candles flickered between them, more for ambiance than light. No one looked up when we approached. But they felt us.

"Elise," one of them exclaimed as he stood. A man with skin like bronze and hair slicked back in perfect, unnatural stillness. His accent was unplaceable. European, maybe. "You brought him."

"He's ready."

They all turned to look at me then—four sets of eyes that didn't blink. Not once.

The one beside the bronze man was a woman with close-cropped curls and a scar that ran from her jaw to the edge of her eye. She smiled wildly, teeth. "He even smells new."

Elise interrupted, "Shut up, Olivia, he's mine."

The third was impossibly young. Barely out of his teens. Pale as frost, with hands that trembled just enough to make me wonder how long it had been since he fed.

And the fourth—

The fourth wasn't seated. She stood at the end of the table, watching me with arms folded across her chest like she already didn't like me. Her gaze pinned me, dissected me, dismissed me. "What's his name?"

Elise didn't answer. She looked at me instead.

I swallowed. "Alex."

The fourth smiled, but it wasn't kind. "Alex, then. Try not to embarrass her. Take a seat."

I didn't respond. I wasn't sure I could. Elise didn't flinch. She slid into the booth, tugging me beside her, her thigh pressed firm against mine. It grounded me.

Elise looked to the bronzed man with the slicked-back hair. "Alex—this is Dracula. Dracula, this is Alex."

I was shocked—stunned. I felt frozen in place. I couldn't move.

Then they all burst out into laughter. He extended his hand toward mine. "Bruce—pleasure to make your acquaintance."

Olivia chimed in, "Dracula has been dead for thousands of years, we're just fucking with you—relax. His name wasn't even Dracula, it was Drake—but you know how time distorts everything."

"These are the old ones," she said, still laughing.

The youngest-looking one interrupted, "Oh fuck off—I'm Lacy."

"Lacy—" I said hesitantly.

"Oh fuck you too then!"

They all erupted into laughter again. The woman with the scar spoke up, "Don't let his name or appearance fool you—he's older than all of us."

Lacy looked to her. "Thank you, Samantha, you all are uncultured swine. Lacy used to be a very manly name in my time. It just hasn't aged well—and Alex, you're no one to cast stones."

I relented. "I'm sorry, I didn't mean anything by it—I'm just nervous."

The bronze man leaned forward. "Have you told him

yet, Elise? They're calling it MIR-4476 now. A fluke. A mutation. But we know what it really is."

"What?" I asked.

He looked at me, and for the first time, I felt something beneath the charm—a rage older than nations. "It's a gift. And they want to kill it."

Before I could ask who they were—who wanted to kill it—the door creaked open.

Not slammed. Not shattered.

Just... opened. Calmly. Like someone arriving early to a funeral.

Three men wearing overcoats walked in. Not Whitby locals. Too clean. Too still. Their eyes scanned the pub like a spreadsheet. No curiosity. Just calculation.

I recognized them instantly as a threat, by their purple aura.

Elise went rigid beside me.

"Don't stare," she said under her breath, and that was when I knew—they weren't here to drink.

Bruce's fingers curled around the edge of the table, just once. "We don't run," he said, almost lazily.

"We also don't die for no reason," Samantha interjected, eyes already following their path.

"They won't start something here," Olivia said, though her voice held doubt. "Too many witnesses."

"They won't start it," Lacy replied. "But they'll finish it if we blink."

I could feel my body reacting before I understood why. Pupils narrowing. Pulse slowing. Muscles tightening like an animal about to bolt—or pounce. I wasn't human anymore. And these men—weren't just men.

They stopped at the bar. Didn't order.

Then I heard it—a soft click. The duffel bag unzipped.

Samantha was already moving when the first one pulled the weapon free. It wasn't a gun. It was worse. Sleek. Silver. Humming low like it wanted to be fired. She tackled him, and they both went down, a blur of limbs and growls and glass shattering.

Then the second man raised his arm and fired.

Not a bullet.

A dart.

It hit Lacy dead in the chest.

He didn't scream. Just looked down, confused, like someone waking from a dream. Then he fell sideways, twitching, foam spilling from his lips.

"Elise—" I grabbed her wrist. "What is that?"

"Curare compound, synthetic serum. Designed to paralyze the gene. Then rupture it."

I couldn't breathe. "They're killing him—"

"Yes."

Bruce was on his feet now, lifting a stool and slamming it across the agent's jaw. Bone crunched. The man staggered. Olivia lunged next, her hands glowing—glowing—with heat. Not fire, exactly, but friction. Her palms tore through Kevlar like paper.

The third agent pulled a knife.

I stood, but too slowly.

He came for me.

Everything slowed. Not metaphorically. Literally. Like time obeyed a different law now. I saw the blade. The wrist behind it. The breath he held in preparation for pain.

Then Elise stepped in front of me.

She didn't dodge. She took the knife.

Straight to the stomach.

She didn't flinch.

Her eyes went black. Not dark—black. She smiled as

she wrapped her fingers around the man's throat and lifted him from the floor with one hand. His boots kicked at the air. His face turned a shade of panic I didn't know humans could reach.

"You touched what's mine," she said plainly—with power.

She snapped his neck like it was an afterthought.

The pub had emptied in seconds. Chairs overturned. Beer pooled at my feet. Glass crunched beneath bodies.

Utter chaos.

Lacy wasn't moving.

I dropped to my knees beside him. His mouth trembled. His eyes had rolled back. "He's not gone yet," Samantha said, crouching beside me. "But he will be if we don't burn that shit out of his blood."

"I don't know how—"

"You do."

Elise didn't move, but her voice carried. "Feed him!"

"He's dying!" I shouted, eyes wide.

"You're not human anymore," Elise snapped. "Act like it."

I leaned in, heart pounding. My eyes scanned the floor for broken glass. My hands grabbed a shard and I cut deep into my wrist before my mind even could think. I pressed my open wrist into Lacy's mouth. I could feel him drinking my blood. A futile animalistic reaction. He stopped shaking. His eyes rolled forward and his hands grasped my wrist. The pressure was intense, a sensation I'd never felt before.

Then he pushed my wrist away. He had a crazed look in his eyes. Like a wolf. Wild. Searching.

"Fucking hell," he rasped. "That... that hurt like shit."

Samantha laughed, close to tears.

I sat back on my heels, blood dripping from my wrist. "Did it work?"

Lacy blinked, then nodded once. The air reeked of scorched metal, synthetic toxin, sweat. I looked around. Three bodies. All still. All dead.

Elise was still stooped over one of the men, feeding.

Bruce leaned against the bar. "This was a message."

Elise called out, "Alex—come eat."

"They've found us," Samantha said. "They know Whitby isn't myth anymore."

"They've known," Elise said. "This wasn't discovery. This was a test."

I drained the last of the life from the only remaining alive man on the ground.

Olivia turned toward me, eyes gleaming. "Now we show them we're not just monsters hiding in the dark."

"We burn their labs," Bruce said.

"We erase their data," Samantha added.

"And if they want war..." Elise stepped toward me, brushing her thumb across my cheek where blood had dried, "then they get it."

She kissed me. Not soft. Not desperate.

Certain.

I could hear police sirens wailing.

Distant at first—just a suggestion, a faint call carried in the wind—but growing louder. Closer. Real.

My stomach dropped. I pulled away from Elise. "Shit—Elise. The police."

"They won't make it in time," Bruce said, already moving, already calm.

"But what if they do?" My voice cracked. "The bodies, the blood—us. CCTV. We'll be arrested. We'll—"

"We won't be seen." Olivia tossed a broken chair aside like it was paper. "Not clearly."

"What do you mean?"

Samantha spoke as she wiped Lacy's face with the hem of her sleeve. "We don't show up right on film. Too fast. Too wrong. Just... blurs. Blips of static. Only our clothes ever really register. Like ghosts wearing coats."

"You're telling me none of this will be clear?"

"No," Elise said, grabbing my hand. "But they'll know. And we need to move. Now."

We didn't leave through the front. Bruce kicked open the back door, leading us into a cold alley framed by old stone and the stink of discarded fryer grease. The sirens were just a block away now, blue lights flashing against brick.

I followed them on instinct—Elise's grip never loosened, even when we ran.

We didn't move like humans. Not anymore. I didn't need to catch my breath. Didn't need to pause. My legs felt mechanical, silent, precise.

We cut through alleyways, vaulted over a low iron fence, and climbed a twisting hill until the noise of the town faded to nothing but our own steps, and the hum of something electric just beneath my skin.

Bruce's house sat at the top of the hill, behind a wrought-iron gate and a towering wall of ivy. It looked... impossible.

Modern, but not sterile. Stone and steel. Hidden floodlights. Long stained glass windows that reflected nothing but were impressive even at night. Like the house had been there forever but was updated with all the creature comforts modern technology had to offer.

A machine waited just beyond the gate—a sleek, black Jaguar with no license plate.

As the rest of us slipped through the side entrance, Bruce scanned a small panel with his palm. The door clicked open. No keys. No guards.

He turned back to me as we entered. "Welcome to obscurity."

Inside was worse—or better. I couldn't tell.

The house was cathedral-quiet. Polished floors, bloodwood stairs, walls lined with books and paintings that felt stolen from somewhere important. The air smelled like sandalwood and ozone and something iron beneath it all.

"This is yours?" I asked.

Bruce smiled faintly. "Mine. Ours. It's been in the network for decades. Maybe longer."

Lacy collapsed onto a leather chaise, arms sprawled. "Remind me never to drink from someone that clean again. Felt like bleach going in."

"Be glad Alex saved you," Samantha added.

I wandered toward a floor-to-ceiling window that looked down over all of Whitby. The sea looked black from here. Infinite. And the Abbey, perched on the cliffs above it, stared back with eyes that refused to blink.

"What the hell was that?" I asked, my voice breaking. "Those men. Why us?"

Elise didn't answer.

Bruce did.

"They weren't just normal murders," he said, shaking his head. "Those bastards are just killers, criminals. This was different. Methodical. Trained. Mercenaries."

"Mercs?" I repeated, still tasting iron. "From where?"

Samantha tossed a towel toward Lacy without looking at me. "Cirgenix."

The name hit like a migraine. Cold. Clinical. Designed to be forgotten—but impossible to ignore.

Olivia turned from the shattered glass. "They're the ones who engineered MIR-4476. Marketed it as a breakthrough in longevity. Claimed it could reverse cellular aging."

"But it wasn't a breakthrough," Elise said. Her voice was steady, too steady. "It was an attempt to play God."

I stared at her. "They're researchers. Why send assassins?"

Bruce knelt at the hearth, struck a match, and touched it to the kindling. "Because they didn't invent the gene. They copied it. Clumsily. What we have—Morbus Sanguiatis—it's old. Real. Surviving it changes you. But they didn't want change. They wanted profit."

"They tried to sell what they couldn't understand," Samantha said. "But the body rejected it. Trial subjects bled out. Or tore themselves apart from the inside."

"They couldn't recreate us," Olivia muttered. "So now they'll erase us—to protect the illusion. And try again."

She threw a photo onto the table. Satellite resolution. Blurry but clear enough.

"Cirgenix," she said. "It's a private company in Roatán. Honduras. Buried in the jungle. Offshore. Unregulated. Untouchable. They built it there for one reason—so no one could stop what they were doing."

"They've already started the purge," Bruce added. "Anyone with Morbus Sanguiatis. Bitten but breathing. Turned but hiding. Entire bloodlines gone."

The room shifted sideways. Or maybe it was just me. The firelight shimmered over the blood drying on my hands.

"And me?" I asked. "Why me?"

Elise didn't hesitate. "Because you're new. Because you crossed the threshold without help. You turned successfully—that's rare."

"And because," Bruce said, "you're visible. You write. People read you. That makes you dangerous."

I turned to Elise, my chest tightening. "What? You told them I'm a writer?"

She didn't answer.

I stood. "How does Cirgenix even know who I am?"

"They don't," she said. "Or—they didn't."

My stomach sank.

"But after tonight," she continued, "they will. You turned. You fed. You lived. That makes you rare. That makes you useful."

It circled in my mind like a drain refusing to empty.

Cirgenix.

A company, an institution playing God.

A machine. Smiling. Godless. Precise.

The kind that doesn't kill out of fear—

It kills because it can't patent what it can't contain.

I swallowed hard. "What do they want?"

Bruce didn't flinch. "Don't be so naive. They want ownership; the original gene—Morbus Sanguiatis—can't be successfully replicated. So they made a counterfeit, MIR-4476, and are trying to perfect it. They need us as lab rats."

"Designed in a lab," Samantha said. "Structured to mimic us. But it's not."

"It's synthetic," Olivia added. "Unstable. Their test subjects either died immediately or rotted from the inside. The body knows when it's been lied to."

"They wanted immortality in a syringe," Elise said. "What they got was a hallway of corpses."

"And now," Bruce said, "they're erasing the truth."

"They only have one lab," Samantha said. "Roatán. Deep jungle. International blind spot. If it burns, no one asks why."

"They started quiet," Olivia said. "Targeted. The ones who didn't even know what they were yet. But now? They're getting desperate."

"They were biotech?" I asked. "Now they're executing people in pubs?"

"They always were," Samantha muttered. "Cirgenix is just the mask. Behind it—military money, private contracts, no laws."

I stepped back from the fire. My pulse was too loud in my ears. "How long has this been happening?"

"Since the Nazis," Elise said. "They were the first ones to find the closest replication. After the war, it died with them—those evil bastards. Cirgenix found it somehow, what they did. Now they're trying to perfect it and sell it to billionaires."

Samantha dropped a folder onto the table. It exploded open—surveillance stills, autopsy diagrams, redacted field reports, names, coordinates. Too many.

"We're not the first," she said. "We're just the first they didn't get to in time."

I sat down hard.

Everything in me felt too loud.

Bruce watched me like he already knew what I was thinking.

"You choose this," he said. "But the moment you turned... the moment you tasted blood... you became a threat to everything they built."

"They won't stop," Olivia said. "Not until we're erased. Down to the last cell."

The fire cracked sharply.

And Elise—Elise was watching me again. Like she had that morning. Unblinking. I didn't look away.

"I need you to understand something," she said, her voice a whisper pressed through steel. "This isn't a war we win by hiding."

"No," Bruce agreed. "But it's one we survive by violence—quick, unflinching violence."

I looked back at the folder. A photo stuck to the inside flap. Grainy. Faded. But I knew it instantly.

I looked at Elise. She didn't blink. Didn't move.

## CHAPTER 10
# THE TEETH IN YOUR MOUTH

Elise stood. Not like she'd made a decision—but like gravity had let her go.

She didn't speak. Didn't look at anyone. Just rose from the chair, slow and deliberate, as if the room had nothing left to offer her.

I stood, too. Instinct maybe. Or delusion. Like something in me still thought I was supposed to follow her. That I was equal to whatever she was.

She stopped in the doorway.

Turned.

And lowered her hand.

Palm down. No words. No force. Just the soft, downward flick of her fingers. A gesture too casual to mean anything—unless you felt it.

I did.

I stopped like my spine remembered something my mind didn't.

A hand found my shoulder—weight. Bruce.

"Sit," he said, quiet.

I did.

She walked out of the room without another glance.

No one followed.

The silence she left behind wasn't awkward. It was devotional. It stretched out, thick and alive, curling at the edges like smoke from something holy—or burning.

Lacy was the first to move. He pulled a half-empty bottle from the table and took a long drink like it hurt to stay still.

"She does that," he muttered, more to the bottle than to us. "When it gets too loud."

"She does it so you'll shut up and think," Samantha said.

"To think about what?" I asked. My voice sounded too loud in the room. Too human.

Olivia smirked. "To remember it's not about you."

"I didn't say it was."

She raised her brows like I'd proven her point.

"She's not whatever you think she is," Bruce said. "She's not your lover. Elise—she's the Bloodline."

"What? Bloodline—what are you talking about?"

Nobody answered.

"She's the Accord," Samantha finally said.

"The Alpha, the Omega..." Lacy murmured into the bottle.

Bruce nodded. "You feel it. You just don't have the words for it. Ironic for a writer like yourself, I bet. But you need to believe it. Now."

"Believe what?"

Lacy's eyes finally moved from the bottle and to mine. "She's life and death. Always has been—always will be. Don't you get it?"

Frustrated, I kicked my chair from beneath me as I

stood and shouted, "For fuck's sake! Get what? Fucking say it!"

Bruce stood and forcefully pressed his hand to my chest. "Cleopatra."

"Cleopatra what?" I yelled.

Bruce swept my legs from beneath me and pushed me to the floor quickly, violently. "She will hear you—lower your fucking voice."

Lacy spoke up. "I think it's a rumor—that she's actually Cleopatra. But rumor or not—we're a part of her story, she's not a part of ours. She's never talked a lot about her past—probably too much to say. I don't know why she picked you..."

"Picked me for what?"

Lacy continued. "You're her first toy in over a century. She hasn't turned anyone for ages."

Still confused, I relented. "What's going on here? What am I?"

Samantha interrupted. "You're a Morbus—just like us. But what you are—that's whatever Elise decides. Elise is the Bloodline—the strongest, the oldest, the original. She was born with the gene. We were all turned. Not by Elise, but by others. The fact that you survived being turned by the Bloodline—don't let it get to your head. But you will see. The way the others look at you... you're one of us—but you're not. You are the only living Morbus turned by the Bloodline—Elise. She is the gene. She is the top of the pyramid. Everything starts and ends with her."

No one said anything after that.

The fire snapped in the hearth, its light crawling up the stone. Lacy stared into his bottle like it held answers. Samantha pulled her legs up into the chair, arms wrapped around her knees. Bruce didn't move. Not even his eyes.

I sat there on the floor, breath shallow, chest tight, blood still humming with everything I didn't understand. I couldn't decide if I was terrified or worshipful.

Both, maybe.

The silence broke when I heard her return—barefoot, deliberate, the creak of old wood beneath her weightless step. She hadn't changed clothes. I had no idea what she was doing upstairs—I couldn't ask.

The air of the room evacuated with inevitability as she entered. Without speaking, we—along with the room—rearranged ourselves around her.

Bruce straightened. Samantha unfolded. Lacy stopped drinking.

And I—

I couldn't get off the floor.

She looked at me for a moment. Not unkindly. Just... as if I were part of the room. Then she turned away.

"We leave tonight."

That was it. No buildup. No plan spilled across a map. Just a fact spoken into existence.

Bruce nodded. "Where?"

"You will see," she said.

Olivia nodded.

Elise looked at her. Just looked. Olivia dropped her gaze.

Elise continued. "No calls. No trails."

Samantha asked, "What if we're followed?"

Elise smiled. "We're always being followed."

Lacy coughed gruffly. "We splitting up?"

"No. Not yet. They want fragmentation. They want the web broken. We stay close—for now."

She turned back to me then. The first time she'd really seen me since the others opened the wound of her past.

Her expression didn't shift, but something in her gaze curled cold around my throat.

"You chose this," she said. "You're either with me, or you're not."

It wasn't a question. It wasn't even a statement. It was an ethereal proclamation that we all already knew the answer to. The cost of it.

I didn't answer. I didn't know how, but she saw through me—my desperate answer in my eyes.

"You don't know what you are yet. But you will. Soon."

She moved toward me, slow. She didn't crouch. Didn't kneel. Just reached out with one hand and touched my face—my cheek, my jaw, the corner of my mouth like she was feeling for something beneath the skin.

"You still think this story belongs to you," she said. "Everything—down to the teeth in your mouth..."

Her thumb grazed my lip, then pulled away.

"They're mine."

The best or the worst part of it all—I loved it. I loved her. I wanted her.

She turned again, her voice already fading with the distance.

"We leave in fifteen minutes. Don't bring anything you're not willing to lose."

Then she was gone again.

The others didn't wait for me.

They started moving—fast, efficient, silent. Like soldiers. Or followers.

No one asked if I was coming.

Because it wasn't a question.

It never had been.

. . .

The door clicked shut behind me.

Fog kissed the threshold—cold and low. The kind that moved like breath, thick with things unsaid. The thing I loved about Whitby.

They were already gathered.

Bruce stood with his arms crossed, shadowed by the edge of the van. Samantha leaned against the side panel, eyes distant, lips drawn. Olivia didn't even pretend not to watch me. Lacy paced a slow circle near the back bumper, his boots heavy in the gravel.

Elise—she stood by the driver's side, shoulder resting against the frame, a cigarette lit and loose between her fingers. She wasn't smoking it. Just holding it. Watching it burn like she was thinking about time.

When I stepped closer, she didn't say anything. Just flicked the pack open with one hand and offered it to me.

I took one. She lit it for me with the cherry of her own, not bothering with a lighter. Our faces were close for a second—close enough I could smell her even through the pungent smoke. I felt synced with her pulse, like an extension of her.

We smoked in silence.

The night didn't move. It felt like it was waiting.

"I don't dream," she said, almost to herself.

I didn't answer.

She glanced sideways. "You still do?"

"Sometimes."

"Keep them," she said, exhaling slowly. "They'll be the last thing that's yours."

The end of her cigarette glowed. Then she dropped it, crushed it with her boot, and looked down the road.

"We're heading south."

"London?"

She didn't nod. Didn't blink. Just started walking.

"Lacy, keys," she said.

He tossed them. She caught them without looking.

"Passenger," she added.

"Like always..." Lacy muttered, already moving.

We climbed in without being told where to sit. Samantha pressed against the window, arms folded. Bruce rode behind Lacy. Olivia slouched deep, head back, headphones in but nothing playing. I slid in last. The door slammed. Elise was already up front.

The van pulled out slow. Tires grinding over wet gravel, headlights halfheartedly eating through the fog.

For a while, no one said anything.

Not until we got to York.

"Don't panic," Bruce said. "But we've got a tail."

Elise calmly added, "I know—let's stop at the Minster. See how far they're willing to go."

Lacy glanced up in the mirror. "Are you sure that's a good idea?"

"Are you sure I asked if it was?" Elise said, flat.

Samantha tensed beside me. "The black Land Rover two cars back?"

"Yeah," Bruce added. "Could just be a drink driver though."

"No," Elise said, quiet. "It's not."

"What do you want me to do?" Lacy asked.

"Keep pace. Go to the Minster."

He did.

The black car behind us dipped once. Then again.

I felt my pulse in my neck.

We could feel them following us. We all just knew somehow.

Elise unbuckled her seatbelt.

"Don't stop," she said.

Lacy opened his mouth—thought better—kept driving.

The window on her side rolled down slow. Cold air sucked in. She lit another cigarette. The wind fought her for it, but she won, of course. She always did. The flare lit her face for a second, and I swear I saw something ancient behind her eyes. Not just age—but memory. The kind that carries wars.

We drove under a stone archway—the kind tourists photographed during the day. Now it looked like a wound in the road.

"We're not stopping," she said again, half to herself, half to all of us.

Lacy tightened his grip on the wheel. I saw the white of his knuckles.

"Are we pulling them into the open?" Bruce asked.

Elise exhaled smoke that whipped sideways out the window. "We're leading them into a trap."

I glanced back. The Land Rover was still there.

Samantha leaned in toward the center. "There's a roundabout coming. If we peel off through the front of the Minster, we can park and they will follow."

So we did exactly that.

Lacy veered off, tires hissing over ancient stone, and we slid to a stop in front of York Minster like it was nothing. But it was something. The kind of something old churches were built to bury. The cathedral loomed above us—limestone bones rising into fog—its stained glass dark, its windows hollowed out by the night.

We stepped out.

Not fast. Not slow. Just... inevitable.

There was a calm that dripped off us. The kind that only happens before blood. Like we weren't walking into a trap—we were the trap.

Samantha, Olivia, Lacy, and Bruce peeled left.

Elise and I went right, beneath the east tower.

I didn't speak. Couldn't. The air felt thick with liturgy and death. Fog moved like breath across the ground. I could smell the iron in the stone. Hear the click of my own teeth when I swallowed.

Then they came.

Four of them. One we didn't see until later.

The first three moved like ghosts who hadn't earned it yet. Civilian clothes. Military steps. Each carried a rifle. Green laser dots licked across the cathedral's skin, climbing toward the heavens like they were looking for God—and didn't like what they found.

We waited.

One heartbeat.

Two.

Elise vanished.

Not a blur. Not a sprint. Just—gone.

The first man let out half a breath before his spine bent backward, his mouth still open when his body hit the ground. The second raised his gun, but Elise was already past him—then behind him—then inside his scream. She snapped his neck mid-turn like she was plucking a stem.

Bruce took the third with a kind of violence that looked akin to a broken love—hard and fast and final. Bone cracked. Air left lungs. Samantha moved beside him, expression still, fingers fast. One sharp jab under the ribcage, another to the larynx. He dropped like his soul had been revoked.

I didn't remember deciding to move. Only that I was on someone's back, teeth in his shoulder, blood in my mouth. His scream started and didn't finish. I tore it out of him.

The world tasted red.

Then I heard it.

A gunshot.

Not one of ours.

Bruce staggered.

He dropped to one knee, then fell.

I turned—saw him.

The fourth. Clean-shaven. Calm. Hidden just outside the perimeter. His rifle still red hot. I could see the outline of the barrel. I could smell the smoke even from here.

He raised it again.

Elise was in front of him before he could breathe. She caught the barrel mid-shot—bent it slightly with just her grip. He tried to scream. There wasn't time for that.

She only looked at him.

He died like something remembered. Like a memory that had nowhere left to go.

And then there was silence.

Except Bruce.

He was bleeding. Bad.

Samantha was already there, pressing her hands to his shoulder. Olivia pulled off her jacket, folded it tight, added pressure. Blood soaked through it like it wanted out of him. She pushed her jacket into the wound.

Bruce cried out, "Fuck! Fucking bastards!"

"Lacy. Bag. Now."

He tossed it to her—rattling metal, gauze, forceps, adrenaline. Her hands worked on memory. No hesitation.

I knelt beside Bruce. He looked at me like I was far away. I wasn't.

"You're fine," I said.

He wasn't.

A lie I felt like I'd told myself a million times before.

Elise stood over us—watching, calm, collected.

"Do it," she said.

I knew what she meant.

I didn't think. Just bit into my wrist.

Pain bloomed, then dulled.

I held it to his mouth. He didn't flinch.

He drank.

My blood. The new blood.

He coughed. Choked. Swallowed. Breathed.

His eyes rolled. Focused.

The color came back to his face.

We stayed like that for a moment. Everyone watching. The street holding its breath.

Fog wrapped around us like a closing fist. Somewhere, the cathedral bells didn't ring.

Elise stood.

"We leave now."

No one argued. No one asked if it was over.

We lifted Bruce together and disappeared into the dark.

The stones didn't remember our footsteps.

But the blood would.

I would never forget.

## CHAPTER II
# ELISE

I didn't sleep. None of us did. Sleep implies safety. Sleep implies distance. There was none.

We fled to a flat just outside Knaresborough, a grey-bricked thing with windows too small and locks too old. But it had walls. It had silence. And for a moment, that was enough.

The others took separate rooms. No one said anything. No one had to. We were bruised in places too deep for blood. And I—

I followed her.

She didn't tell me to. She didn't have to.

Elise stood in the doorway of the smallest room at the back of the flat, her silhouette carved out of moonlight. She didn't look at me, not fully. Just stepped inside, expecting the air to follow. I did.

The bed was narrow. The kind built for utility, not want. But she turned and peeled her shirt from her shoulders like it was the most natural thing in the world. Like I hadn't watched her kill. Like I wasn't still shaking from the sound of gunfire and blood hitting stone.

I undressed slower. Not from hesitation—because it felt like a ritual. Because being naked in front of her wasn't exposure. It was reverence.

She didn't climb into bed. She climbed onto me.

There were no words.

Only breath. Heat. The friction of something too powerful to name. Her hands pressed my wrists into the mattress. Her mouth traced across mine like a signature. I didn't move—not because I couldn't, but because I didn't want to. Being beneath her wasn't weakness. It was the only place I made sense. There was no place I'd rather be.

We didn't make love.

We unmade it. Tore it down to its bones and rebuilt it as something rawer. Hungrier. Sacred and violent all at once. I couldn't tell where I ended. I didn't want to. Every sound from her mouth was a command I was born to obey.

She was fire. And I—I didn't burn. I opened.

When it was over—if it ever really ended—she rolled off of me and lit a cigarette. Her skin still held the thin fleeting warmth of us, but her expression had gone distant. The flame caught on the end of the cigarette and bloomed like a red eye in the dark. The smoke curled up toward the ceiling, delicate, dangerous.

I watched her. Like I always had. Like I always would.

The silence between us grew until I couldn't breathe.

So I broke it.

Softly. Hesitantly.

"What are we?"

She didn't answer.

Not at first.

She pulled smoke into her lungs like she was filling a well that had no bottom. Exhaled slowly. Carefully. Like the question was fragile.

"Was this..." I paused. "Was this something you needed to get out of your system?"

Still, she said nothing.

But her body changed. Not visibly. Not in any way a stranger would notice.

But I wasn't a stranger.

I saw the tension in her mouth. The curve of something sharp beneath the softness. She let the silence drag. Let it eat at me.

The first one to speak loses.

And I lost.

"I love you."

She closed her eyes. Just for a second. When she opened them, they were unreadable.

"I love you too."

But the words hung in the air like the smoke. Lovely. Suspicious. Fleeting.

A lie that tasted too beautiful to question.

I wanted to believe it.

Needed to.

She turned her head toward me finally. The way a lion might look at something it's already claimed. A kill it's already staked.

"You already know what we are," she said.

"Then say it."

Her gaze held mine. And held it. And held it.

"I didn't just choose you," she said. "You chose me. But you didn't know it then."

"And if I had?"

"You would've run. And I would've let you."

"But I didn't run."

"No." She reached out and touched my throat—barely. "You knelt."

"So tell me." My voice cracked. "What are we?"

Her smile was slow. Not warm. Not cold. Just true.

"The worst kind of thing."

"Which is?"

"Soulmates."

I didn't speak.

"You're in me now. And I'm in you. There's no going back from that."

"Is that love?"

She leaned in, kissed me once—chaste, cruel.

"No," she said. "It's necessity—it's fate. There's no way out from teeth like mine."

I came to hate my skin. I shivered. And not from cold—I am the cold. I am the benefactor of those that turn the horses into glue.

"You still don't know what you did, do you?"

"What I did?"

"That night. The pub. You opened something. You called. And I heard you. You invited me in. I was waiting—and you couldn't resist. Humanity. It's absurd. You may have been a writer—but this story—our story—is mine. I decide when it started—I'll decide if it ends."

"I didn't know I was calling."

"But I knew." Her voice dropped to a whisper. "I've been waiting for you. Through centuries. Through wars. Through every version of this world that tried to forget me. You didn't exist. And then you did. And now you always will."

She placed her palm flat over my heart.

"You belong to me."

"And you?"

She didn't hesitate.

"I never belong."

I took the cigarette from her hand, pulled in a long drag.

One that would make you want to slip your skin. Feeling the brief rush—chasing a dragon.

I exhaled, "And still," I said. "I'm yours."

Her nails grazed my ribs. Slow. Gentle. Dangerous.

"And I'll break you," she said.

"No, you won't."

"And you'll thank me."

I'm losing my mind—I think it's for real. I close my eyes and tell myself to be calm—but what is that?

She curled into me like a vice, her breath hot against my skin.

And I let her. Not because I didn't have a choice—but even if I did, it would be her. It would be this.

Because I didn't want to remember who I was. I didn't want to be who I was.

Be calm.

This wasn't romance.

This was ruin.

And I loved her for it.

I pushed out a smile.

What was the point of it all?

For a long time we lay there, neither of us moving, the sheets a twisted knot around our legs, the smoke hanging between us like a nightmare you didn't want to wake up from—lost in limbo. Somewhere in the flat a floorboard creaked and the old pipes groaned, the small sounds of a dying house. Outside, wind pressed against the glass, rattling the frames.

It would have been easy to let my eyes close, to pretend, just for a heartbeat, that this was something ordinary. Two bodies tangled in the dark, the afterglow of sex softening the edges of everything ugly. But that lie was too small to fit us.

My mind kept running back to what she'd said.

Soulmates.

It sounded so benign, something carved into tree trunks and scribbled in notebooks. But in her mouth it tasted like prophecy. Not a vow. A verdict. Something older and colder than romance.

I thought of my life before her—of drunk nights and failed manuscripts, of mornings when my biggest worry was whether anyone would read the words I bled onto pages. I tried to see those days clearly, to call up faces and laughter, but they felt like photographs left in the sun. Faded. Sepia. Fragile. If I reached for them too hard, they'd evaporate to dust.

What had I been then? A writer? A son? A man with options? The night in the pub—I chose her. Lost in limbo.

The idea that she had seemed to be a character dropped into my story seemed, suddenly, inevitable. As if every choice I'd made had been a breadcrumb dropped on a path I didn't know I was walking. As if every woman I'd thought I'd loved had been a rehearsal for this ruin. As if, somewhere inside, I'd been calling out for something wild enough to consume me. Maybe she was right. Maybe I'd invited her in long before I knew her name.

I wanted to ask her what she remembered. Cleopatra. Bloodline. The Accord. Those names swirled in my head like myths and warnings. Had she loved like this before? Had she laid in beds in Rome or Alexandria or London watching another man watch the smoke curl from her lips? Was there a path worn into her heart by centuries of footsteps? Or was every connection singular, a thread pulled taut between two souls until it snapped? I wanted to know. I was terrified to know.

My hand drifted toward her, slow, a reflex more than a

decision. Her skin was cool, not human warm, but there was still a pulse at her wrist. One that now matched mine. It thrummed. It vibrated through her like the low hum of something electric. She didn't flinch when my fingers brushed her. She let me touch her, let me map the line of her collarbone, the curve of her breast. But she did not reach back. Her hands were her own, resting on her stomach, a cigarette balanced between two fingers like a little stick of waiting. I felt like I was tracing the surface of a weapon. Beautiful, deadly, alluring.

"You said you've been waiting for me," I whispered, the words almost lost in the sound of her exhale.

"Yes." Her voice was a shadow of itself. No less sharp. Just softer around the edges.

"How did you know it was me?"

Her head turned on the pillow, and for the first time since she'd pinned me to the bed her eyes met mine without that distance she used like a shield. For an instant there was something almost human there—something like an ache.

"I felt it," she said. "Like a missing piece. Like a tooth searching for its root."

"You could have taken anyone."

"I did." She smiled without humor. "I took everyone. And none of them were you."

The room seemed to shrink. The ceiling tilted closer. A log in the fireplace downstairs cracked and collapsed, sending up a soft hiss as embers shifted. I wanted to say more. To ask if she'd feel me if I died. If she'd know if I tried to run. If she would follow. If I wanted her to. The questions spun in my head like moths around a light.

She rolled to her side, pressing her body along the length of mine. A lazy claim, an assertion of dominance and something more. Her hair spilled onto my chest, dark and heavy. Her breath warmed my skin. Her hand found my ribcage again, fingers splayed over the place where my heart used to live. She could probably feel the difference. The way my pulse faltered and stuttered now, catching up to the new rhythm the gene had written inside me.

"I will break you," she murmured again, not as a threat. As a promise.

"You can't," I breathed.

We lay like that until the cigarette burned down to the tired filter and the ember singed her fingers. She crushed it in the glass on the nightstand. The room smelled like ash and sweat, like sex and old paper. Eventually, she slept—or something like it. Her breath went shallow, her weight heavier.

I didn't. My eyes stayed open, watching the pattern of the cracked plaster on the ceiling, the way the light shifted as the streetlight outside flickered. My mind slipped sideways, back to the fight at the Minster. To the way Bruce had gone down. To the look in his eyes when he came back. Grateful. Horrified. I wondered what he thought of me now. If he thought of me at all.

When I couldn't stand the stillness anymore, I slipped out from beneath her. She made a sound, low and annoyed, but did not wake. I pulled on the jeans I'd dropped by the door and stepped into the hall.

The flat was dark except for the weak light leaking from under a door near the front. It smelled like cheap cleaning solution and damp stone. I padded down the hall, past the closed doors where Samantha and Olivia and Lacy had presumably retreated. Bruce's door was cracked. I pushed it open.

Samantha sat on a chair beside the bed, her feet tucked

under her, arms wrapped around her knees. She looked exhausted, her braid coming loose, her shoulders slumped. Bruce lay on the mattress, shirtless, his shoulder healed, his skin grey with blood loss. He was sleeping—actually sleeping—his mouth slightly open, his brow furrowed even in rest.

I guess even the dead rest, after all.

Samantha looked up when she saw me, her eyes sharp in the half light. "You should be with her," she whispered, not unkindly.

"I—needed... air," I stammered back. I nodded toward Bruce. "How is he?"

"He'll live." She sounded like it was more curse than comfort. "Thanks to you."

I didn't answer. Shame and pride twisted together in my stomach. We'd saved him, yes. But he was hurt because of me. Because I was the bait. Because I had insisted on pulling them into the open. Because I'd asked the questions.

"You love her," Samantha said, not a question.

"You say it like it's stupid." My voice was flat.

"It is." She leaned forward, her elbows on her knees. "It's stupid and it's inevitable and it's going to kill you. Maybe not now. Maybe not for a century. But it will. We've all loved her. In our own ways. We all still do. It doesn't matter."

"Then why warn me?"

"Because I like you." A ghost of a smile crossed her face. "And because sometimes pain tastes different when you can see it coming. It can be your fantasy."

I laughed softly. It sounded more like a cough. "Do you regret it?"

She looked at Bruce, at the way his chest rose and fell.

At the thin line of sweat on his brow. "Every day," she said. "And no. Never."

We sat in silence for a moment. The house creaked. Samantha stood, stretching her back. "Get some rest," she said. "We move at dawn."

"Where?"

"London, Heathrow," she answered. "We're taking the fight to them. Their headquarters. Their labs. The nest."

The word pulsed in my head. Nest. As if this was all an infestation, a hive, something alive and spreading.

"Do you think it's safe?" I asked.

She laughed, a short, dry sound. "No. That's why we're going."

Back in the bedroom, Elise hadn't moved. She slept like a statue, like something carved. I climbed back in beside her, not touching her, feeling the chill of the sheets. My thoughts whirled, but my body was lead. Eventually, I must have slept, because when the door opened and the morning light seeped in grey and thin, I flinched like I'd been shot.

"Up," Lacy called, voice gruff. "We're burning daylight."

I dressed in silence. Elise moved with me, measured, indifferent. There was no softness left from the night before. She was all angles and inevitability again. We met the others in the small kitchen. Olivia's hair was braided tight, her jaw clenched. Bruce stood, pale but upright, a clean shirt hiding his scar. Samantha shoved a half-full duffel bag toward me.

"Carry this," she said. "And don't drop it. It's for emergencies."

"What's in it?" I asked, hefting the weight. It felt like metal and glass and dread.

"A deterrent," Bruce muttered. "And an invitation, if we need it."

Outside, the fog had thinned but not lifted. The van waited, its white paint streaked with dirt. The dawn's light burned—but just briefly. Elise went straight to the driver's seat. It felt like a pattern already. We pulled away from the curb without looking back. The flat, the grey-brick walls, the narrow bed where I'd been unmade—all of it vanished into the rearview mirror.

Miles slid under us. Fields gave way to motorways, and the sky went from pewter to steel. No one spoke much. Music would have felt obscene. The only sound was the hum of the engine, the occasional click of Elise's turn signal, the wet slap of tires on asphalt. My thoughts spiraled in the silence.

I looked at Elise, the way her hands wrapped around the steering wheel like it was alive. I wondered if she felt the same pull I did. If this bond she'd named was as new to her as it was to me, or if she'd said those words a hundred times to a hundred lovers who'd all thought they were the one. I wondered if any of them had gotten farther than this. I wondered if I would.

When we passed the sign that read LONDON 188 MILES, a low buzz filled the van. It wasn't the engine. It was something under our skin, a tremor that ran from person to person like an unspoken rumor.

Elise reached out without looking and rested her hand on the center console. Her fingers brushed mine, just a graze, a promise. The road ahead was long and straight and lined with possibilities that tasted like gunpowder and ash. Somewhere in that sprawl of city and history, the heart of this thing beat. And we were driving straight toward it.

"This is the last quiet we'll have," Samantha said, breaking the spell. "Enjoy it."

I pressed my forehead to the cool glass of the window

and watched the hedgerows blur. I thought about fate and choice and everything Elise had said. I thought about the taste of her mouth, the iron tang of blood, the hum under my skin that didn't belong to me anymore. I thought about the word soulmates and how it sounded like salvation and damnation in the same breath.

I thought about the end of this road. Not the asphalt, but the line she'd drawn between us and whatever waited in Roatán. I didn't know if we would all survive. I didn't know if I would survive her. But for the first time, the uncertainty didn't feel like fear. It felt like a prayer.

As the van ate up the miles and the grey horizon of London drew closer, I closed my eyes. In the darkness, I could still see her. Not as a woman. Not even as a monster. As a gravitational field. As a truth I'd stepped into and couldn't step out of. Love, ruin, fate. They were all words for the same thing.

Better dead than in hell.

I smiled, just a little. The kind you make when you know you're about to do something irreversible.

## CHAPTER 12
# CRUMBLING DOWN

Luckily you saw something in me, something I couldn't see. It sounded like a line from one of my novels, but it was Elise's voice in my ear as the van ate up the motorway. She said it so matter-of-factly, as if she were recounting the weather, not the reshaping of my life. If anyone else had said it, it might have been comforting—an assurance that I was worth saving. From her, it was a reminder that my value had always been hers to define.

The sun was just starting to lift over the hedgerows when the road widened and the first planes appeared overhead, white bellies flashing in the grey. Heathrow loomed in the distance, a glass and steel hive already humming. We were cutting it close on time, not because of traffic—we'd left early enough for that—but because nothing about us went unnoticed anymore. A late change of plans could derail everything.

"Remember," Samantha said quietly as the terminal grew larger in the windshield. "No heroics. No fangs. We're tourists. Brain-dead with travel fatigue. We pass through like everyone else."

"Brainless," Lacy muttered, half to himself, his jaw tight. "Right."

Elise didn't acknowledge him. Her eyes were fixed on the lanes of cars sliding into the departure drop-off. Her hands relaxed on the wheel in a way mine never did. She looked like she could have been driving to a coffee shop, not to a war.

"You saw something in me," I repeated under my breath, as if saying it twice might make it less strange, less terrifying. She glanced at me, a corner of her mouth hitching, and then pulled the van into a narrow gap by the curb.

"Everyone out," she said. "Take only what you need. Carry yourself like you belong here."

We spilled onto the pavement with duffels and backpacks, blending in with the families and business travelers and bleary-eyed tourists. The blast of jet engines and the hiss of buses and the buzz of voices washed over us. The hunger that had been a low hum since York rose up like a wave, taller, sharper. I could smell everything: the acrid bite of exhaust, the sharp citrus of an orange, musky suitcases, passersby... It was unbearable and intoxicating. My teeth ached.

"Focus," Elise said, her voice barely audible. She didn't touch me, but the word pressed down on my pulse like a thumb. "We've done this before. You will not lose control."

Inside, the terminal was a cavern of glass and light. Departure boards flickered with destinations—New York, Dubai, Barcelona, San Pedro Sula. We joined the line for check-in, weaving between retractable belts with the patient shuffle of cattle. Olivia's fingers drummed on her passport, her eyes scanning the crowd. Bruce's face was drawn, a sheen of sweat at his temples. Lacy muttered under his breath. Samantha kept her gaze on the woman ahead of her, a mother wiping yogurt off a toddler's mouth.

When we reached the counter, we stepped forward in pairs. Olivia went first with Lacy. He slid his passport across the desk, his fake name and fake profession smiling up from the laminated page. The airline employee smiled back. For a moment, I thought this would be easy.

Then Bruce handed his passport over.

"Sir," the agent said, her voice too bright, "I'm sorry, it looks like there's an alert on your booking. Could you step to the side while I get a supervisor?"

His jaw tightened. He shot Elise a look. She gave nothing away.

"We don't have time for this," Samantha murmured, too low for human ears. "They're going to pull him into secondary."

Elise stepped forward, placing her hand on the counter as if she belonged there. "Excuse me," she said, her tone polite, almost bored. "We have a connecting flight. There must be a mistake."

The agent blinked. Her gaze slid from the screen to Elise's face and stopped. She didn't look away. For a heartbeat, I saw the full weight of Elise's attention coalesce. It wasn't a power like in the stories—no flick of a wrist, no shimmering eyes. It was worse. It was the complete conviction that you were the only thing she'd ever focus on. The agent's breath hitched. Her posture slackened. Her fingers hovered over the keyboard, waiting for permission.

Elise smiled. Not wide. Just enough.

"It's my fault," she continued, the lie rolling off her tongue as truth. "I made a last-minute change to his itinerary. We're traveling together. Surely you can see we're all just trying to get to our holiday. Wouldn't want to disappoint us."

The woman's mouth opened and closed. She nodded once, slowly, like a puppet. "Of course," she said. "Of course. I... must have misread. It's not a problem."

I felt the hair rise on my arms. Samantha exhaled. Lacy's shoulders lowered a fraction. Bruce's jaw unclenched. The agent typed something, stamped our boarding passes, and waved us through. When we walked away, she blinked rapidly, frowning, as if she'd lost time.

"How in the hell did you do that?" I murmured, falling into step beside Elise.

"Charm," she answered. "I'm irresistible—it was just a nudge. Enough to tilt the scales. Too many eyes here for anything else. You will learn it too—all good things come in time."

We wound our way toward security. The line stretched long and serpentine, people stripping off belts and shoes and watches, placing laptops into grey bins. My heart rate spiked. I'd always hated airports—the vulnerability of it, the way strangers rummaged through your belongings, the metallic smell of anxiety. Now, with the gene awake in me, everything was amplified. The woman three places ahead must have been pregnant; her blood smelled different, thicker. The man behind us hadn't showered; stale sweat clung to his clothes. Somewhere down the line, someone had cut their finger on a zipper; the faint drip of blood set my hunger on edge.

"Control," Elise reminded us, without moving her lips. I nodded, grateful for the warning and hating that I needed it.

Elise went through the metal detector first without any issue.

Then it was my turn.

I stepped forward, trying to mimic her calm—but as I passed through the archway, the machine screamed to life. A sharp, metallic chirp. I froze. The security agent raised a hand.

"Step back, sir. Empty your pockets."

I felt the heat creep up my neck. I turned out my pockets, showed my belt, nodded toward my shoes. Then I realized.

My watch.

Fuck.

I reached down and unfastened my vintage Rolex from my wrist—the one I never took off. The one Elise had told me I no longer needed. It felt stupidly heavy in my hand now. I set it in the plastic tray like I was laying down a weapon.

The agent's eyes landed on it. Then narrowed.

"Sir," he said, "is this yours?" Picking it up to inspect it. "Rolex Oyster Perpetual Ref. 5552..." Pushing down the band a bit to expose the serial number, "13118789." He said aloud.

"Obviously—you watched me take it off," I said, too fast.

Holding it with two fingers by the edge of the bracelet. "Do you have documentation for this?"

"What?"

"Receipt. Appraisal. Import declaration?"

"No, I—why would I carry a receipt?"

He turned it in the light. "This is vintage. Possibly pre-Air-King. Rare. You have an American passport. You don't have proof of ownership?"

"It's mine," I said again. "It's been mine."

He gestured, and another guard came over, this one

with a clipboard and a more serious badge. I glanced over at Elise—already through, arms crossed, waiting. Her eyes met mine. They were not amused.

"Where did you purchase it?" the second guard asked.

"A dealer in the States," I said. "Private sale. Years ago."

They conferred, muttering about customs thresholds and duty tax, whether the piece should be seized for verification. The watch sat there in the tray, inert, exposed. I hated how naked I felt without it. I hated that they were touching it. I hated that I didn't listen to Elise.

And then Elise stepped forward.

"Gentlemen," she said, her voice dipped in something honeyed and dark. "We're about to miss our flight."

They looked up at her. Both of them. Like dogs hearing a whistle.

She smiled. "The watch stays with him. There's been no theft. No declaration needed. He's simply—American... don't hold it against him."

"Well that's for me to decide, innit?"

"Well of course—but you can forgive that, can't you?"

For a moment, neither moved. Then the first man blinked, shook his head like waking from a trance, and slid the Rolex back toward me.

"Fine," he muttered. "Just... next time, declare it."

I slipped the watch back onto my wrist, pulse hammering.

Elise leaned in close as we walked past the checkpoint, her voice low and sharp in my ear.

"Your fucking watch," she hissed. "I told you you didn't need that fucking watch."

"I forgot," I said.

"You didn't forget. You're still fucking wearing it."

I didn't argue. She was right.

And I hated that she was always right.

Our bags slid through the X-ray one by one. The duffel Samantha had insisted I carry went in last, nonchalant, a bag full of clothes and nothing dangerous to the untrained eye. The security officer frowned, looked closer. His hand hovered over the conveyor belt.

"Is there anything sharp or liquid in here?" he asked, eyes flicking to me—again.

"No," I said. "Just clothes." My voice didn't tremble. I could have convinced myself.

He opened the bag. I watched his hand dive into the dark, brushing past neatly folded shirts. His fingers closed around something cold and cylindrical.

For a moment, he held it up.

It was a metal thermos. He unscrewed the lid, sniffed. Water. He looked at the lid, the inside, the empty void. He handed it back, uninterested. "Fine," he said, waving me through.

On the other side of security, we gathered, breathing shallow. Olivia was pale. Lacy rubbed his temples. Samantha's eyes darted between the exits and the giant digital clock overhead. Elise looked bored, as if the whole charade had been beneath her.

"It seems like the only place time matters is here."

"Gate B42," Bruce said, reading his boarding pass. "We board in twenty minutes."

The walk to the gate felt endless. Every step ached—we were all hungry. We needed to feed. Every announcement about final calls sounded like a verdict. I couldn't stop cataloging people—shuffling toddlers, elderly couples, businessmen with their neck pillows. They had no idea what we were. They had no idea that "monsters" were moving among them, clutching coffee and boarding passes. They were ignorant of the danger, and for the first time I envied them. To live in a world where you could walk through an airport and only worry about missing your flight felt like a fairy tale.

At the gate, we sat in a row, our knees touching, our backs to the glass. Outside, planes taxied, their engines coughing to life. Raindrops speckled the windows, blurring the view. An advertisement on the wall showed a smiling couple on a white beach, cocktails in hand, promising paradise. My life felt like the negative of that image. Now with Elise—it was a sinful heaven.

When boarding was announced, we moved with the crowd, scanning barcodes, nodding at attendants, slipping into the jet bridge. The sudden change in temperature, the scent of recirculated air—it all made me dizzy. On the plane, we had three rows, window and aisle seats. I took a window, my knee pressed to Elise's thigh. Across the aisle, Samantha sat between Lacy and Olivia. Bruce slid into the row behind us, pressing his shoulder to the window, his eyes already closing. He needed the rest more than any of us. He was still weak, I could smell it.

As the plane taxied, my stomach flipped. When it lifted, my ears popped. The pressure made my teeth ache. I closed my eyes and focused on breathing, on not listening to the seventy-plus heartbeats around me. It was like sitting in a church and trying not to hear the congregation. Impossible.

"I know it hurts," Elise said softly, as the seat belt sign dinged off. "It'll pass."

"It feels like..." I couldn't find the words. "I can hear everything."

"You can." She leaned close, her lips almost brushing my ear. "Use it. Listen to them. Hear how small they are. Let that be the leash on your hunger. You're not them anymore. You're not meant to be. You are mine."

It was the first time she'd acknowledged the difference between us in that way. It should have frightened me. It thrilled me. I leaned back, letting the sounds wash over me —the soft rustle of magazines, the click of plastic cutlery, the murmur of movie dialogue, the slow, rhythmic breathing of a sleeping child. In the middle of it all, I found a steady heartbeat. Strong. Slow. Familiar. Elise's. It anchored me like a lighthouse.

I looked over to Elise. I needed to know.

"Before we go into this—what am I?"

She took my hand in hers before turning towards me.

"Do you want to know the truth? I don't think you can handle it."

I nodded, "I can—I do."

She inhaled the recirculated air deeply.

"You—are a muse. A desire—a thirst. One that I don't want, one that I can't refuse. To me, it's shameful to admit —that I want you. I don't want anything—I have everything, at least I thought. When I saw you in that pub, I knew exactly what you wanted.

We are a fatal attraction.

I'm not good for you. You're not good for me; but I couldn't stop myself. Honestly, I hoped you wouldn't turn. I hoped you would die like the rest of them. But—something inside me, something knew too. Knew that that wasn't the truth. Knew that you were the only thing that could scratch that itch. The one inside of you that you push out of your mind...the guilty pleasure, the version of you that you repress because you know it's wrong. And that—that's exactly why you want it so much. You know nothing about me, but you love me to death. Did you ever stop to ask yourself why?

You are the only tie to me and mortality. You are my è guǐ."

I didn't understand...

"...è guǐ?"

"The hungry ghost..."

"È guǐ," she repeated, and kept her eyes on the window where our reflections sat doubled in the oval. "Hungry ghost. People use it to scare children or excuse adults. That's not what it is. It isn't a superstition and it isn't a specter. It's a shape created by need—an emptiness that learns to feed itself by choosing a body to orbit."

Her words moved with a careful economy. She spoke like a surgeon cutting around something vital.

"Think of it like this," she went on. "The human body has hungers—salt, sugar, sleep, touch. They rise, they're met, they fall. Then there's the other kind—the one that survives satisfaction. My hunger—my truth. You feed it and it grows teeth. You starve it and it grows a tongue. It isn't desire for a thing. It's desire for the feeling that desire gives—heat, recognition, the charge of being seen. That's è guǐ. Not a ghost in the room—a geometry in the self."

I breathed through my teeth, slow. The plane shivered and settled. Somewhere behind us ice clinked in a plastic cup.

"It anchors to memory," she said. "Always. That's the first rule. Something half-remembered—a smell, a sentence, a pair of eyes across a crowded place, the taste of an afternoon you thought would never end. It hooks there. Second rule—once it anchors, it requires a living proxy. It will choose someone and say 'There. Feed me with that.' The person becomes a well. Every glance a sip. Every refusal a deeper thirst. The more you try to behave, the more it teaches you to hunger."

I felt myself leaning toward her without moving—pulled by the clean edge of her voice.

"Third rule," she said, quieter. "È guǐ doesn't want you happy. It wants you wanting. It wants the ache. It will mimic love because love keeps you near the well. It will mimic art. Faith. It will learn the grammar of whatever you worship and speak it back to you until you kneel. That's why people call it a haunting. It keeps returning in the language you can't refuse."

She turned then. Not coy—steady. "You are mine," she said, unornamented. "You are my hungry ghost."

The hum in the cabin seemed to thicken. I swallowed. "Explain."

"I wouldn't expect you to understand—not yet," she said. "You're too fresh. Your blood still believes in edges. But listen anyway." She placed her hand on the closed tray table between us, palm down. A neutral touch that wasn't a touch. "I have taught myself every discipline. To take and not take. To fast. To feed and stop before the stopping turns into the need for more. I have worn other people's hunger and folded it neatly away. I don't blush at desire. I don't beg. I have learned to live where the river is strongest and step out dry."

Her mouth tightened. A muscle in her jaw flickered and was gone.

"Then you walked into a pub with rain on your collar, and it wasn't your mouth or your hands or your voice. It was the thing behind them—the damage you carried like a lit room. Your soul is as fucked up as mine. I didn't want it. I can't refuse it. È guǐ recognized itself in you and chose. That's what it does. It chooses a mortal tether and says—

this one. Through them, I will remember what warmth meant. What danger felt like. What morning did to the eyes."

I couldn't make my hands unclench. My nails bit my palms. I said, "So I'm a symptom."

"No," she said, and the word cut clean. "You're the vessel. You're the one absence can drink from without spilling. Don't cheapen it. Don't aggrandize it either. It isn't romantic. It isn't noble. It's accurate."

She let the silence settle until it had weight.

"When I say you are my è guǐ," she continued, "I mean the hunger in me has taken your shape. I mean my restraint fails along the outline of your mouth and the color of your tiredness. I mean when I shut my eyes, the idea of you is more nourishing than blood. And I hate it. And I would kill it. And I can't. Because killing it would mean losing the last instrument that plays any audible note in me."

I breathed, once, and it hurt the way cold air hurts a healed wound.

"Listen to the mechanics," she said, and there was something almost clinical in her tone now—kindness of a different sort. "It lives in the gap between sensation and meaning. Touch becomes proof. Absence becomes proof. It metabolizes both. If I kiss you, the ghost grows because it has tasted you. If I refuse you, the ghost grows because you become more idea than body—more myth than skin. The ghost thrives either way. That's why moderation fails. That's why vows fail. That's why people ruin themselves and call it fate. The universe is rigged toward wanting."

"Can it be starved?" My voice sounded smaller than I felt, especially over the plane's engine roar. The question embarrassed me. It left me exposed—child at the edge of a well.

"Yes," she said, and did not make it a comfort. "But starvation doesn't cure it. Starvation turns it clever. It will volunteer to be 'healthy' so it can survive you. It will wear your better angels and repeat your rules back to you until you trust it again. Then it will suggest one exception. One drink. One night. One last time. The old language returns, fluent, persuasive, tender. And you will call the relapse a reunion."

I stared at our hands—hers still, mine trying to be.

"Now the part you don't want," she said. "È guǐ is never only one thing. It multiplies into the corners. You become my ghost—I become yours. You start to guard the absence the way I do. You start to prefer the ache to any resolution. You'll call it devotion. You'll call it art. You'll write pages meant to heal you and be furious when they do, because healing starves the very reason you wrote."

The engines rose and fell through a pocket of rough air. The seatbelt sign flicked on. We didn't move.

"You asked for truth," she said. "Here is the last piece. È guǐ is older than our genes. It predates any lab, any monastery, any bed. It waited inside our kind for the first story that felt more necessary than food. That's why it recognizes me. That's why I recognized you. I can survive on blood. I cannot survive without a reason to keep waking in a body I did not choose. You are that reason. Not because you're good for me. You're not. Not because I'm good for you. I'm worse. But because the hunger chose your outline as the only shape that could convince me I still belonged to the world of breaking and mending."

She turned her face fully to mine then, and there was nothing predatory in her expression. Only fatigue. Only clarity that cost something.

"You wanted me to say you were special," she said.

"Fine. You are. But not the way you imagine. You are special to the appetite. You are beloved by the part of me that wants to be human without paying for it. And you will suffer for that adoration, and so will I, because adoration that refuses cost is only another word for consumption."

I felt something inside me sit down and look at its hands.

"What do we do with it?" I asked.

"The better question is what will it do to you," she said. "We don't dress it up. It learns our routes—how it moves through our mornings and our work and our nights. We give it water, not wine—not blood. We name it when it shows up wearing your face or mine. But we have no power to deny it the drama it needs to breed. We cannot refuse the spectacle. We are the spectacle. We are the disaster, and together or not, nothing will separate us."

She let her words breathe in a silence that consumed me. Then, softer—almost human again. "And sometimes we feed it on purpose, because starving always breaks what it's meant to spare. We choose the feast and accept the sickness that follows. We don't call the sickness love."

I thought of the first night. The taste of iron and salt and rain. The shock of being wanted with no explanation. The relief of it. The grief.

"You are my hungry ghost," she said, like a benediction that didn't promise anything. "That means when I look at you I remember the weight of daylight on a kitchen table. I remember the sting of laughter I didn't have. I remember my mother's hands. It means when I try to leave you, the hunger will rattle its cup and I will want to run back and press my mouth to your throat until the world goes uncomplicated again. It means both of us are in danger of mistaking annihilation for intimacy."

She reached up and adjusted the vent above her, a click, a sigh of air on my forehead. A small, ordinary kindness. Then she rested her hand near mine—close, not touching.

"You wanted a sentence to carry out of this plane and keep," she said. "Here."

She held my gaze, and for a moment I saw it—the woman behind the want, the ledger of costs paid and promised.

"You are the part of us that loves hunger more than it loves what hunger wants," she said. "You are where mine wears a name."

Her hand hovered near mine on the armrest, the air between us still trembling from what she'd said.

For what seemed like a long time but was probably only a few seconds I chewed on her words, I couldn't speak. Not because I didn't understand—but because I did. Too well.

When I finally found my voice, it came low.

"My father used to tell me a story," I said.

That made her turn, just slightly, like she wasn't sure whether to mock me or listen. I kept my eyes forward.

"It begins with water," I said. "Still at first—reflecting nothing, only existing. A shallow pool cupped in darkness, waiting for light to find it."

Her eyes caught mine as I looked towards her; she didn't interrupt.

"Then motion," I went on. "A slow slosh against stone. Ripples folding into themselves. And above the pool—faces. The soft blur of hair leaning over the edge. Eyes glinting, mouths moving with laughter or hope. Then hands—hands releasing something small and bright."

I could hear his voice as I spoke, slow, deliberate, the way he used to tell me bedtime stories he didn't believe in.

"The coins fall through the air like moments too heavy

to hold," I said. "Each one strikes the surface and disappears, sending out a pulse that fades and folds back into the dark. And the pool—he said—it absorbs everything. The wish, the want, the confession. It takes them in and keeps them. Over time it stops being clear water. It becomes memory. Weight. Desire made physical."

Elise was staring at me now. Not moving. Not blinking.

"My father said that's the mistake people make," I continued. "They think they're the ones wishing. They think the well is listening. But that isn't how it works. The well isn't passive—it's alive. It feels every coin strike the surface. Every need. Every plea. Until one day it understands. It understands because we are the wishing well itself."

Her lips parted slightly. "Understands what?"

"That it's not the watcher," I said. "Not the one who wishes. It's the water. The stone. The well itself. It's where wanting goes to rest."

I looked down at my hands, the tremor in them, the faint crescent marks from my own nails.

"He told me that once you understand you're the well," I said, "you stop trying to fill yourself with people. You stop trying to drink from them. You realize you were never empty—just carrying everyone else's need. And if you can let go of it without drowning, that's what makes you human."

Her eyes softened, almost painfully. "He sounds like he understood hunger."

I nodded. "He did. He just never had a name for it. Not like yours—not like mine—our hunger."

Something flickered in her gaze—fear, maybe. Or reverence.

I turned to her fully then. "You called me your hungry ghost. But you're wrong, Elise."

Her breath hitched. "I'm never wrong."

"I'm not the ghost," I said. "I'm the well. The place your hunger comes to die, or to sleep, or to be forgiven—I don't know which. You feed on me, and I let you, because somewhere in me there's a piece that still believes that's mercy."

She said nothing. The plane dipped through a pocket of turbulence, light flashing across her face like lightning through small panes of glass.

"My father said the well never asks the water to stop falling," I whispered. "It just learns to stay still enough to let it pass. That's what I'm doing with you. I'm not fighting the hunger anymore. I'm embracing my truth—you."

Elise closed her eyes. "That's worse," she murmured.

The hum of the engines deepened through the clouds below, faint lights scattered like lost stars across the coast.

"He told me something else, before he died," I said quietly. "He said something I didn't understand at the time, until I met you—the real miracle isn't that the well gives water. It's that it never stops reflecting the sky, even when it's full of the dead's wishes."

Her eyes opened. Wet. Sharp. Almost human.

"That's what I am to you," I said. "A reflection that remembers the sky. Not your salvation. Not your curse. Just the thing deep enough to show you yourself—whatever that may be. We are two lost souls—broken, deserted, dead. That's why we are here—that's why we are together."

The plane steadied, engines easing into a low, tired whine. For a long time, she didn't answer. Her hand finally moved—only an inch—but it was enough.

Her fingers interlaced over mine, and she murmured, "Then if there is a God, let her help the both of us."

I looked at her and almost smiled.

"She already has," I said. "She gave us the hunger."

Hours blurred. We flew west, and time warped. I watched a landscape of clouds shift from grey to pink to nothing. I watched the sun set and rise during the flight. I thought about what awaited us in Honduras. I thought about Cirgenix, about their lab hidden on an island. I thought about the Purples, the mercenaries who'd been hunting us. I thought about what Samantha had said the night before: the nest. My stomach knotted with something that wasn't hunger. This was bigger than my obsession with Elise. This was bigger than my transformation. We were about to tear down the thing that had made us and kill the people who wanted to harness it. War wasn't hyperbole. It was fact.

When the captain announced our descent into San Pedro Sula, my hands were trembling. The humidity hit us the moment the plane doors opened. Warm, wet air that smelled like earth and ocean and diesel rolled down the jet bridge. The airport was smaller than Heathrow, a single terminal with tiled floors and a low ceiling. The signs were in Spanish, the colors brighter. I tasted salt on my tongue, not just from the sweat beading on my lip.

Customs was a row of glass boxes with men in uniform leafing through passports. The line moved slower than Heathrow's. I could feel my patience thinning. Elise stood behind me, her breast pressed lightly to my back, her breath at my neck. Every muscle in my body felt tight. Every voice around us was louder. Olivia tugged at her shirt collar. Lacy wiped his palms on his jeans. Samantha rubbed her thumb along the seam of her passport. Bruce leaned heavily on the handle of his bag.

When it was my turn, I smiled at the officer. His

name-tag read Jorge. He had the round, tired face of someone who'd processed a thousand travelers. He flipped through my pages, found the stamped entry from London. His eyes flicked up at me, then down again. He asked a question in Spanish I didn't catch. I shook my head. He tried English.

"Purpose of visit?"

"El turismo," Elise said, stepping forward as if she were bored again. She wore a white linen shirt, sunglasses perched on her head despite the dim lighting. She looked like every wealthy European who'd come to Honduras for beaches and ruin. "La playa. La selva. Los tiburones. Ver todo." Beach, jungle, sharks. See it all. She smiled, showing a sliver of teeth.

Jorge's pupils dilated. He nodded, scribbled something on the form, and stamped our passports. No questions about our bags. No interest in our itinerary. When Samantha stepped up behind me, he didn't even look at her. He stamped and waved. We were through.

We paused just past the sliding doors, the heat like a wall. A chaos of drivers with signs and families hugging and vendors selling phone cards pressed in. The sky beyond was a burning blue. I tasted the air. It was thick with exhaust and distant salt. Underneath, faint but unmistakable, was another scent: blood. Not the sterile, processed smell of airport terminals. This was warm, running, alive. My throat tightened.

"You all smell that?" Lacy asked, his voice low.

"Yeah," Samantha answered. "Keep it together until we're clear."

Elise's eyes tracked across the parking lot. "We'll rent a car," she said. "Then we feed. Not here. Too many cameras. Down the road, there's a turnoff. We'll find what we need."

Need. Not want. Need. It felt clinical. It was clinical. We were addicted to life, and life tasted like blood.

The rental car desk was another queue, another sweaty exchange of paperwork and keys. Another moment of breath-held patience. Then we were outside, throwing our bags into the back of a dusty SUV. Bruce slid behind the wheel, his shoulders rolling back. He'd always been the one to drive when things were dangerous. Perhaps it made him feel in control.

We pulled out of the lot and onto a two-lane road bordered by sugarcane and billboards for mobile service plans. The sun was a fist overhead. Sweat beaded down my spine. Bruce drove with one hand on the wheel, the other resting on his bandaged side. Samantha sat shotgun, maps open on her phone, watching for turns. In the back, Elise took the middle, one hand on my thigh, her nails digging in just enough to remind me she was there. Lacy stared out the window. Olivia scrolled through news headlines on her phone. I tried not to look at the veins in Bruce's neck pulsing with his heartbeat.

After ten minutes, Elise said, "Here."

Bruce turned down a narrow dirt track lined with scrub trees and high grass. We bumped over rocks, branches scraping the sides of the car. The road opened into a small clearing where a rusted corrugated hut leaned, half-collapsed, the door hanging off one hinge. There were tire tracks in the dirt, beer bottles half-buried, cigarette butts in the grass. The smell hit me full force then: sweat, adrenaline, cheap cologne. And underneath it, fear. Human fear. Fresh.

Lacy clicked his tongue. "Locals. Might be a gang spot. Perfect."

Samantha shot him a look. "Don't be a psychopath."

He shrugged. "Better us than them. And they're likely armed."

Bruce killed the engine. "We feed quick. We don't leave evidence. We don't get shot. Everyone clear?"

We nodded. It felt ludicrous to be discussing feeding on criminals like planning a picnic. But there was nothing else to do. We were too weak to storm a biotech lab if we didn't feed. Hunger wasn't a choice. It was a hunger that would drive us to kill each other if we let it.

We stepped out into the thick, humid air. Flies buzzed. A cicada whirred. We moved as a unit, Elise at the front, me at her shoulder. Samantha to the left, Lacy to the right. Bruce and Olivia flanking. The ground was uneven. My shoes sank into mud. I could hear voices behind the hut—male, laughing. The sound of a slap. A feminine yelp. More laughter. The smell of stale beer. Anger flared in my chest. It wasn't righteous. It was selfish. The thought of their warm blood in my stomach was electric.

Elise held up a hand. We stopped. She stepped around the hut's corner like smoke. I followed, blood roaring in my ears.

There were three of them. Two leaned against a car, their shirts open, tattoos snaking down their chests. One had a girl pressed against the hood, his hand on her throat. Her eyes were wide. Her lip was split. She couldn't have been more than sixteen. They didn't see us until we were on top of them.

Elise was on the one holding the girl first. Her hand clamped over his mouth. Her other arm wrapped around his neck. She pulled him backward, away from the girl, his eyes bulging. She sank her teeth into his throat with a precision that was almost tender. He convulsed. She drank. He sagged.

Samantha had the second man, her forearm against his jaw, her fangs sinking into the soft skin at his shoulder. Olivia and Lacy took the third together; he swung, but they were faster, dragging him behind the car. Bruce pushed the girl toward the trees. "Run," he whispered in Spanish. She stumbled, barefoot, and vanished into the brush.

I had a man too—someone I hadn't seen in my first scan of the clearing. He came out of the hut, a pistol in his hand, curse on his lips. He raised the gun. I was on him in a breath, my hand on his wrist, twisting until the bone cracked and the gun fell to the dirt. His other hand clawed at my face. I didn't feel it. My mouth found the curve of his jaw. Heat. Salt. Metal. Life. It spilled into me, hot and thick, and the ache under my ribs eased. My muscles flooded with strength. My vision sharpened. The fevered static in my mind went quiet. The world narrowed to the throbbing of his pulse slowing, then stopping.

When I stepped back, he crumpled. My lips were wet. I wiped my mouth on the back of my hand. It came away stained. I watched Elise straighten, her eyes closed, blood on her chin. She looked sublime. Terrible. Infinite. She wiped her thumb across her mouth, catching a drop, licking it clean. The other bodies lay limp, their throats torn, their blood slick on grass and gravel. The clearing smelled like copper and soil and sweat.

"We should go," Samantha said, voice steady but low.

"Cars can be traced," Olivia added, her breath quick. "Phone signals. We have to be careful."

"We will be," Elise said, turning to me. Her eyes were darker now, pupils swallowing iris. Her voice was calmer. Sated. "You need to learn to stop before they do. It's sloppy otherwise."

I nodded, ashamed and glowing.

We dumped the bodies into the rusted hut, out of sight, dragging them by limbs. We didn't look at their faces. We didn't say a prayer. We didn't owe them anything. They were fuel. They were choices they'd made that led them here. They were an excuse we needed.

Back in the SUV, the air conditioning blasted stale cool against our damp skin. Bruce started the engine. The whole thing had taken minutes, but time felt elastic. The hunger had been a gnawing hole; now it was a slow burn, manageable. It made my tongue heavy. It made my limbs heavy. It made me feel both powerful and powerless to it. As we pulled back onto the main road, I felt Elise's hand find mine in the dark of the backseat. She laced our fingers. Her skin was still cold—but alive again. Or maybe mine was colder. She squeezed once, not soft, not hard. Just a squeeze.

"Roatán," she said, speaking the name of our true destination for the first time. The island, the lab, the source. "We end it there. But it's almost daybreak, we need a hotel."

## CHAPTER 13
# UNTIL I COLLAPSE

The hotel wasn't a choice. It was a surrender. One that none of us truly could admit to.

By the time we saw the sign—faded blue letters, half the bulbs dead, cockeyed above a row of sunburnt palms—my vision had started to white out at the edges. Elise's knuckles were bone-pale on the wheel. Sweat soaked the collar of her shirt. The sky was no longer a color, just light, pressing down on the windshield until it felt like the air inside the SUV was thick enough to chew.

"We stop here," Elise said.

It wasn't a suggestion. It never was.

The lot was a slab of cracked concrete scattered with oil stains and plastic cups. The building itself looked like it had been left out in the rain too long—peeling paint, rust bleeding from every metal edge, curtains hanging crooked in the windows. A plastic banner promised air conditioning and free Wi-Fi like those were acts of God.

When I opened the door, the heat hit me like a fist.

It wasn't just temperature anymore. The sun peeked over the horizon, wanting to show itself again to the world.

It felt personal. It made me angry. My skin prickled. The muscles in my jaw locked. Every heartbeat in the parking lot—the front desk clerk behind the glass, the maid dragging a cart along the hallway, the kid crying somewhere on the second floor—beat against my skull like a hammer. The part of me that had fed in the clearing wanted to go back out into the road and drag the whole world into the shade and drink it dry. Make them feel what I felt.

"Move," Samantha said quietly, coming around the back of the car. "We're burning."

I nodded, but my legs didn't get the message right away. They felt wrong—overfilled, like I'd been poured into them too fast. Elise's hand closed around my wrist. Her grip was cool, decisive.

"Inside," she said. "Now."

The lobby was worse. Fluorescent lights hummed overhead, burning into my eyes. The floor was polished tile, off-white and too reflective; I could see the smear of blood at my collar in the shine before I wiped it away with the back of my hand. A television bolted to the wall played some local morning show—hosts laughing too loud, teeth too white. A ceiling fan turned lazily, pushing hot air around in circles.

Bruce handled the check-in, his Spanish almost passing as fluent. The clerk barely looked at us. We were just another group of tourists who'd taken an overnight flight and come down here to lose themselves on a beach for a week. If he noticed the tension in Bruce's shoulders or the deadness in Elise's eyes, he didn't let it register. I don't think he cared.

My hearing kept expanding. The click of keys on the computer. The humming of a neon beer sign. The slow drip of a coffee pot behind the counter. Somewhere in the building, someone coughed wetly, again and again, lungs rattling. I cataloged every sound without wanting to. I hated it.

I put a hand on the reception desk to steady myself. It didn't help.

"¿Estás bien?" the clerk asked, finally looking at me.

I opened my mouth, but nothing came out.

Elise stepped in. "Él no duerme en los aviones," she said, in that soft, reasonable tone she used when she was three seconds from violence. "Vuelo largo. Estará bien cuando se acueste."

The man laughed like that explained everything. Maybe it did.

I had no idea what they said; I didn't care either. I did have a strange feeling though—almost like déjà vu—that I'd been here before, even though I knew I hadn't.

The keys hit the counter with a clatter and broke me out of it.

The clerk went on speaking, but I didn't understand Spanish. I looked to Elise. "What?"

She translated: "Three rooms, second floor. Stairs at the end of the hallway. Breakfast from six to nine. Pool closed for maintenance…all of it useless information."

She seemed annoyed I asked.

"Thanks—sorry."

She nodded.

We made it halfway down the hallway before my body quit.

It wasn't dramatic. There was no Hollywood collapse, no outstretched hand, no infamous last word. One step I was moving, the next my knees turned to water. The carpet came up faster than it should have. The walls tilted. The air vanished.

I heard Elise curse in a language I didn't recognize. Her arm slid around my shoulders, taking my weight before I hit the floor. My vision tunneled, sound stretching into a high, thin thread.

"Alex." Her mouth was at my ear. "Stay with me."

I would have laughed if I'd had breath for it. I'd done nothing but stay with her since Whitby. Since before Whitby. Since the moment she walked into that pub and cracked my life open like a bottle.

The light burned through the thin curtains at the end of the hallway, turning the dust in the air into glitter. It hurt to look at. It hurt not to. Every instinct I had screamed for dark, for cold, for concrete, for earth.

"I'm fine," I tried to say. It came out as a rasp.

"No, you're not," Samantha snapped from somewhere behind us. "We pushed him too hard. We should have stopped sooner."

"We didn't have the luxury," Elise said. Her voice was steady, but I could feel the strain in her grip. "Open the door."

A key turned. A lock clicked. The world narrowed to the rectangle of shadow inside the room.

I let myself fall into it. This time Elise let me hit the floor.

She went about the room, closing all the curtains, blocking out all windows, anywhere light could spill in.

I heard her footsteps grow closer as she walked toward me, then felt a kick. "Get up, stop being dramatic."

"I'm not," I croaked.

I crawled to the place I expected the bed to be on all fours.

"Take off your clothes, they're filthy. You're not getting into any bed with me like that."

I sat on the floor at the edge of the bed and struggled to get my shirt off.

Elise sighed and walked over to me with her wrist outstretched. "Drink."

My teeth sank into her wrist immediately. Instinct.

I felt myself coming back together. She slapped the back of my head and retracted her arm. "That's enough. Better now?"

I shook my head. "I'm going to take a shower."

"That's the first good idea I've heard from you all night," she said with an ominously playful smile.

I pushed myself up. This time my legs obeyed. The room steadied instead of tilting. The cheap art on the wall—the washed-out watercolor of some generic beach—stopped breathing. I crossed the stained carpet and shouldered the bathroom door open.

The light flicked on with a reluctant buzz. The bathroom was as tired as the rest of the place—square white tiles gone grey at the grout, a mirror mottled with old cleaners, a shower stall boxed in by glass cloudy with permanent steam ghosts. I twisted the handle until the pipes groaned and water spat from the shower-head.

Cold.

It hit my chest like a confession.

I stepped under it and let the water sheet down over my head, along my spine, over the dried sweat and borrowed blood and airport skin. Cold like the day in Whitby when the wind had come in off the sea and erased every thought but its own. Cold like something that didn't care if I existed.

I inhaled. The gene in me hummed its disapproval and then, reluctantly, relaxed.

Behind me, the door opened.

She didn't knock. Of course she didn't. The air shifted

around her—pressure, not temperature. I heard the soft sound of the room door closing, a pause, then the lighter click of the bathroom door as she shut us in together.

"I thought you were going to be dramatic and drown," she said.

"I'm hard to kill," I said, water flattening my voice. "You made sure of that."

A beat of silence. Then the faint rustle of fabric. Buttons sliding free. The faint climbing of linen over skin. She undressed like she did everything else—no hesitations, no performance. The performance was built into the fact that she didn't care if I watched.

I saw her in the fogged edge of the glass—just outlines, the suggestion of shoulder and hip. It was enough.

The shower door slid open with a dry scrape.

She stepped in behind me.

The shower was barely big enough for one normal person. For the two of us, it was absurd. Her body came up against my back, not pressed, but near enough that the cold water ricocheted off me and hit her in a staccato pattern. Her hand settled on my shoulder, fingers firm, grounding.

"Before you start thinking that you're about to get lucky," she murmured, "we are only showering."

"I wasn't. You and I both know I don't think," I said.

She laughed. "You were," she corrected. "That's your problem. You turn everything into story. Even this."

"This qualifies," I said. "You in a motel shower in Honduras the day before we storm a biotech lab is objectively narrative."

Her breath huffed against the back of my neck—half disbelief, half something like reluctant amusement.

"You're insufferable," she said.

"And yet."

"And yet," she repeated quietly.

Her hand slid from my shoulder up the back of my neck. It was a practical motion, cleansing, but my body didn't care about the distinction. Every nerve she brushed woke up. The bruises under my skin, under my ego, went quiet.

"You feel better," she said. Not a question.

"Your blood's—different," I answered.

"I know. You took more than you needed."

"You offered more than you meant."

Another pause. The water beat down, relentless and honest.

"I never offer more than I mean," she said.

"Then you meant it."

She didn't answer. Her fingers dug in slightly at my scalp, tipping my head back into the stream to rinse the last of the airport and the clearing from my head. The water seared cold across my face; my eyes closed automatically. In the darkness, with her hand on me, for one brief second it was almost possible to pretend this was normal. A hotel. A shower. A woman who cared if I made it to morning without splitting in half.

Almost.

"Turn around," she said.

I obeyed.

The cold hit my spine instead of my chest now. Elise stood in front of me, close enough that the water cascading off my shoulders hit her breasts and ran down the lines of her body in clear rivers. Her hair clung to her neck in dark ropes. Droplets clung to her lashes, trembling with each blink.

"Look at you," she said quietly.

"Like what you see?" I tried.

She tilted her head, studying me the way she might

study a new scar. "I see a man who almost collapsed in a hallway because he wouldn't admit he was breaking."

"Plenty of people collapse in hotel hallways," I said. "Usually they've just had better minibars."

The corner of her mouth lifted, slow. "Humor as deflection. Classic."

"Violence as deflection," I said. "Equally classic."

Her hand came up, knuckles brushing the side of my throat where someone's fingers had scraped me in the clearing. She wiped away a thin line of dried blood the shower hadn't taken yet.

"I told you you were sloppy," she said. "You killed him too fast."

"Too fast?" I said. "Am I supposed to enjoy it? I mean, he was a person, just like the rest of us—"

Elise cut me off. "Us? You're not a human anymore. I've never been—they're not us. We are all animals; we're just a different breed. But yeah—you should have enjoyed it. Who wouldn't enjoy erasing an evil person from this Earth? There's one less shit-bird walking around and he finally served a real purpose, one that didn't involve making someone else a victim. So yeah—you should enjoy it."

"That's a fair point," I said, just loud enough over the water.

"What restraint," she murmured. But there was no real reprimand in her tone. Only knowledge. We both knew what hunger did when you were stupid enough to give it a human shape.

Her palm flattened briefly against my chest, right over my heart. I knew she could feel it—slower now, steadier, but still too loud in my own ears.

"You're not going to faint again," she said.

"You sound disappointed."

"I'm adjusting my calculations."

"About what I can handle?"

"About what I'm willing to risk," she said.

The way she said it sounded less like tactics and more like confession, but before I could push, she let her hand fall away and stepped back just enough to break the contact.

"Finish up, there's not enough room for both of us in here," she said. "Before you turn pruny and sentimental."

"You joined me," I reminded her.

She rolled her eyes. "You were about to overthink basic hygiene into a metaphor. I intervened."

"That's love," I said lightly.

Her expression flickered. Barely. But I saw it.

"Get out, Alex," she said.

If anyone else had said it, it would have been mundane, an order. From her though, it carried everything—I hung on every one of her words. It didn't matter what she said, what she was even talking about.

I stepped out first, water streaming off me onto the cracked tile. The bathroom's air felt warmer than the shower. I grabbed one of the thin towels from the rack and dragged it over my shoulders, down my arms, along my ribs. It smelled slightly moldy, used and washed over and over again. The mirror reflected a fogged-over, distorted version of me. Before, I hated mirrors—hated seeing the unvarnished truth of myself, eyes too bright and skin too flush. Now mirrors held only truth—whatever stood behind us, and the faint, groggy silhouette of what remains.

Elise stepped out after me, unhurried. She took the other towel and wrapped it around herself in a motion that shouldn't have been modest and somehow was. Not because she was hiding—because she was choosing what to reveal and when. Even in a motel bathroom with mildew in the corners, she moved like someone who'd seen gods kneel.

For a moment my eyes went to the broken mirror so I could catch a glimpse of her. Just for a moment. She noticed.

"See—it's things like that."

"Things like what?" I interjected.

"That show you still think like a normal person and not like one of us. You and I both know damned well our reflections are different—incomplete. And yet you still looked anyway, trying to catch a glance."

Then she turned away, leaving me with my shame.

We put on what passed for clean clothes—me in a pair of shorts and a T-shirt that still smelled faintly like the drawer they'd lived in back in Whitby, her in underwear and the same linen shirt, now buttoned only halfway. It hung off one shoulder, her collarbone exposed.

The air conditioner ran at full throttle, rattling in the wall, doing its best to cool a space that didn't want to be tamed. The curtains were drawn tight. The cheap lamp on the bedside table cast a weak amber circle that didn't reach the door.

Outside, I could hear the others settling. A door closing down the hall—Bruce's, by the heavy footfalls. Another—Lacy's, followed by the muffled thump of him dropping onto the bed. Olivia's voice, low and clipped, through the wall as she spoke to herself like she always does. Samantha's pacing—two lengths of her own room, then the creak of the mattress as she finally forced herself horizontal. Our whole little army, spread along the same strip of hallway like a vein.

One room for each of them.

Ours was the only one with two bodies inside.

Elise crossed to the bed and pulled the covers back with a flick of her wrist. "Get in," she said. "Top your list of firsts: didn't die, didn't get arrested, didn't bleed out on a Honduran hallway. Don't ruin the streak."

I slipped under the sheet. The mattress was thin but it held. She came around the other side and slid in next to me, the bed dipping, our bodies rolling fractionally toward the center. There was nowhere not to be near her.

We lay on our backs at first, not touching, staring up at the cracked plaster of the ceiling. The AC still cried out. Somewhere on the road outside, a truck downshifted, then faded into distance.

"What's the plan for tomorrow?" I asked.

She exhaled, slow. "We get to Roatán."

"That's a destination, not a plan."

"We have a man with a boat," she said. "He knows the currents, he knows the dock, he knows where Cirgenix keeps its fences low. We meet him at the port, we go to the island, we end the problem."

"What's his name?"

She was quiet for a fraction too long. "Don't worry about that."

"Why not?"

"Because knowing it won't keep you alive," she said. "And it will give you something else to fixate on when you should be sleeping."

"You're avoiding specifics," I said.

"And you're hungry for them," she replied. "You think if you understand every step you'll have control over how it breaks. That's not how the real world works."

"That's what you taught me," I said. "Ask questions. Count exits. Know who's on whose leash."

"That's for battle," she said. "This is the night before."

"You're always precise about logistics," I said slowly. "Every time. You love details. You lick them clean. Now you're vague. 'A man with a boat.' 'We end the problem.' That's not you."

She turned her head on the pillow to look at me. Her eyes in the low light were almost colorless, all pupil, all black.

"You think I'm hiding something from you," she said.

"I don't know. Are you? Are you leaving something out on purpose?"

"Should I be—would it even make a difference?"

"For you, yes," I said. "You usually prefer the ugly version of the truth."

She watched me, unmoving. The silence stretched until it felt like another person in the room.

"You know everything that you need to," she said finally. "Conversations I've had without you. Contingencies Samantha and I built into the plan. You want all of it because you think knowledge will keep you safe. It won't. It will only crowd your head. You need your head clear."

"So you get all the weight," I said. "And I walk in blind."

"You don't walk in blind," she said. "You walk in with me."

It was meant to reassure. It didn't.

Something under the words felt off-kilter. Not wrong, exactly. Tilted. As if the floor between us had shifted a degree and I was the only one who'd felt it.

"Elise," I said, "if there's something about tomorrow that changes my part in this—"

"There is," she cut in.

I went still. "Then tell me."

"You're going to live through it," she said.

"That's not information," I said. "That's prophecy."

"It's my intention," she said. "Sometimes that's the only difference."

"Intention doesn't stop bullets," I said. "Or gene therapy. Or Purples."

"No," she agreed. "But it decides who you're willing to put in their way."

There it was again—that slant. The ghost of a cost she wasn't naming. A shape moving in the corner of the plan I wasn't allowed to look at directly.

"Stop," she said, softer now. "You're doing it. You're climbing inside the machinery and trying to see where it will fail. You'll stay up all day running scenarios and none of them will prepare you for the one we actually get. That's the old part of you—kill it or it will kill you."

"That's how I survived before you," I said. "I wrote the worst case, and then I lived through something smaller."

"You weren't surviving," she said. "You were rehearsing your own death sentence and calling it discipline."

"Big words from someone who literally kills for balance."

"Exactly," she said. "I know the difference."

I turned my head toward her. "Then what are we doing right now?"

She watched me for a long moment. Then she rolled onto her side, facing me fully, the sheet pulling with her, fabric rustling against my stomach. The distance between us shrank to inches. Her hand slid up, resting on the pillow between our heads, fingers splayed. It would have taken nothing—half an inch—for either of us to close the gap.

"This," she said, "is the only part I don't know how to plan for."

There was no seduction in her tone now. No cleverness.

Just fatigue, and something underneath it I'd never heard fully unclothed.

"You're pivoting," I said, but my voice came out too low to carry any real accusation. "We go from boats and fences to—this."

"This is the part that matters to you," she said. "If I talk about the plan, you'll pick it apart until dawn. If I talk about us, you'll still pick it apart, but you'll stay in the bed while you do it."

"You think this is a distraction," I said.

"No," she said. "I think you're owed something before I drag you any further into the war I made for you."

A knot tightened in my chest. "What am I owed?"

"The same thing you've been asking for since Whitby," she said. "In a dozen different languages. In every lie you've told yourself about why you stayed."

"Enlighten me," I said.

She swallowed. Her eyes didn't leave mine. I could hear her heart—the slow, controlled beat of something that refused to admit it could still race.

"When I met you," she said, "I thought you were going to be convenient."

I huffed out a breath. "Romantic."

"Don't interrupt," she said, almost gently. "I thought you'd be like the others. A mouth to feed, a mind to admire for a season. A little living proof I could still pass. I walked into that pub thinking about nothing except how you'd taste and how easily you'd disappear."

"I'm flattered."

"You should be," she said. "I chose you over a room full of warmer options."

Somehow that did flatter me.

"But then," she continued, "you opened your mouth.

And what came out wasn't pretty. It wasn't noble. It was wreckage. Held together by habit and a prize people kept reminding you you'd won."

"The Pulitzer," I said.

"The curse," she corrected. "I saw it on you like a noose around your neck. The way you looked at your own hands, like they belonged to someone whose work you were sick of. You were already bleeding when I found you. All I did was give the wound a name."

"Morbus Sanguiatis," I said.

"Not that one," she said. "The other one. The one you can't hide in Latin. The ache you call art. The wish to be ruined by something you chose instead of by something that happened to you."

The room felt smaller. The air between us thickened, full of the memories of every night we'd circled this without touching it.

"You told me on the plane that I'm your hungry ghost," I said. "That the ache in you took my shape. You meant it. I believe you. But you also said I was special to the appetite, not to you."

"I lied," she said.

The word landed between us like a dropped knife.

"You don't lie," I said.

"I lie constantly," she replied. "To everyone. To myself. To the people I've killed. To the ones I didn't kill and should have. The only one I've been trying not to lie to is you. And I failed."

My throat went dry. "When?"

"Every time I told you this was only hunger," she said. "Every time I framed you as an addiction instead of an answer."

The floor inside me shifted. "An answer to what?"

"To why I stayed," she said. Her voice thinned, turned surgical. "To why I keep waking up. To why I haven't walked into the sun just to see if it will finally do what nothing else has managed."

"Elise—"

"You made yourself the well," she cut in. "On the plane. You took my metaphor and broke it open and made it yours. You said you'd hold the ache instead of choking on it. You said you'd stay still and let the coins hit the surface. You thought you were just being poetic. You weren't. You were volunteering."

"For what?" I asked.

"For me," she said simply.

Silence pressed against my eardrums. The world outside honked and hissed and moved. In here, everything held its breath.

"You're not my muse," she went on. "That was the first lie. You're not just my hungry ghost. That was the second. Muse is safe. Ghost is safe. They're metaphors. They keep you at a distance. They let me believe I can feed and step away clean."

"And you can't," I said.

Her jaw worked. "I don't want to."

There it was. Naked. A choice, not an inevitability.

"Elise," I said, barely more than air.

Her gaze flickered to my mouth, then back to my eyes. She was too controlled for her heartbeat to jump, but I heard a microscopic hitch in her breath. A single thread pulling loose from the seam.

"I am—" She stopped. Swallowed, as if the words tasted wrong. "I am not built for declarations. I watched empires fall before most people had learned the word for love. I have seen what it does to people who mean it, and I committed to never being one of them again. It makes you predictable. It makes you soft. It makes you make plans that hinge on wishes instead of weapons."

"You're stalling," I said softly.

"Yes," she said. "Because once I say this, I don't get to take it back. Not from you."

My chest felt too tight. "Say it anyway."

Her hand moved—finally, fully—closing over mine between us. Her fingers threaded between mine, cool and sure, as if this grip had existed long before the bodies it belonged to.

"Alex," she said, and there was nothing in her voice but rawness. No wit. No blade. "I love you."

The room didn't spin. No orchestra swelled. The world didn't pause to acknowledge it. It just landed. Simple, declarative, in a mouth that had never wasted language on anything that wasn't absolutely, terribly true.

I'd imagined this moment a hundred ways. In none of them did she look like this—eyes ringed with exhaustion, hair still damp from a motel shower, shirt misbuttoned, the faintest tremor in her thumb where it pressed against my knuckle.

My voice abandoned me.

She watched the silence pool between us and didn't flinch away.

"I love you," she repeated, quieter. "Not as metaphor. Not as symptom. Not as a flattering description of obsession. I love you in the stupid, human way that makes people ruin good plans and die badly. I love you in the way that made me bring you here instead of leaving you in Whitby where you might have grown old and resented me from a distance."

Her fingers tightened around mine.

"And I hate it," she added. "I hate that it's you. I hate that you walked into my life already broken enough to understand me. I hate that you volunteered to be the well and now I don't know how to drink without drowning you."

My heart hammered so hard I could feel it in my gums. "You're telling me this now," I said slowly, "the night before we walk into...the night before we might die."

"Yes."

"Because you don't want to die without having said it?"

Her gaze sharpened. "Because you don't get to go into tomorrow thinking you were only ever a convenient vessel for my hunger," she said. "You deserve to know the exact scale of the mistake I've made with you."

"Loving me is a mistake," I said.

"Of course it is," she said. "You're terrible for me. I'm catastrophic for you. There is nothing redemptive about this. It doesn't make either of us better. It just makes us honest."

There was something else under her words. A current I couldn't see fully, only feel—the way the air shifted when I asked about the plan, the way she had sidestepped names and routes and contingencies and gone straight for this.

"You're still not telling me something," I said quietly.

Her eyes flickered, just once, toward the door. It was tiny—half a glance—but I caught it.

"I told you the part that matters the most," she said.

"To me," I said. "You told me the part that matters to me."

"Yes."

"And to you," I added.

Her jaw clenched.

"And to me," she conceded.

Her eyes went flat, then softened so fast it almost made me dizzy.

"Stop," she whispered. "Not tonight."

"Elise."

"Do you really want to lie here in this bed, with my love finally in your hands, and choose to pull at the one thread that will unravel the only good thing we get before morning?" she asked. "Is that truly who you want to be?"

I hated that she was right. I hated that she had positioned it like that, framed my suspicion as ingratitude, my need for truth as a refusal of grace.

It was manipulative. It was unfair. It was her.

And despite the jagged edge of doubt in my ribs, despite the sense that some part of tomorrow had already been bargained away without my consent, I found myself loosening my grip on the questions.

For now.

"I love you," I said.

She didn't answer at first. She leaned in instead—slow, deliberate, as if crossing a line she'd sworn never to touch. Her mouth met mine, a brief, devastating press, cool and certain, the kind of kiss that felt less like affection and more like a signature.

When she pulled back, her breath pushed my cheek.

"I know," she said. "I love you too."

Her lips parted. Her eyes searched my face like she was memorizing the man she had decided to ruin.

My free hand came up, hovering near her face, not quite touching. I wanted to hold her, to anchor us both, to keep her from slipping away. Instead I let it hang there, half an inch from her cheek, the air between us hot with everything that might have happened if we were different people.

Her eyes closed, just for a second, like the words hurt.

She shifted, closing the tiny gap, pressing her forehead to mine, effectively cutting the sentence in half. Her hand moved to the back of my neck, fingers resting there as if they were holding me in place.

"Sleep," she said. "We'll talk about the plan when the sun's down again."

Tomorrow.

I fell under with the taste of her admission on my tongue and the sick, beautiful certainty that loving her was going to be the last truly human decision I ever made.

# CHAPTER 14
# NO GRAVE CAN HOLD MY BODY DOWN

The boat was smaller than I'd imagined. That was the first wrong thing.

It sat low in the black water, paint scabbed off in long curls, hull stained the color of old teeth. The outboard motor looked like it had been bolted on as an afterthought. A bare bulb dangled on a frayed wire over the center bench, throwing a sickly cone of light across the wooden planks. Everything smelled like diesel and salt and rotten fish.

The man beside it lifted his cigarette without looking at us. The ember flared, lighting the deep lines cut into his face.

"You're late," he said.

His Spanish was thick with the coast. I understood every other word, more from tone than vocabulary. Elise stepped forward, hoodie up, sleeves rolled, hands empty. Nothing about her posture was threatening. Nothing about it was safe.

"Currents changed," she said. "We're here. Let's go."

He looked past her, counting us. One, two, three, four,

five, six. His gaze snagged on me for half a second, then moved to Bruce, weighed his shoulders, then to Samantha's gear, the coils of wire and black tape and her backpack full of other people's secrets. Lacy hung back, hood up, jaw set. Olivia had her arms crossed tight over her chest, eyes on the water.

"You bring too many," he said. "They hear more, smell more. Dogs, cameras..."

Elise reached into her pocket and held out a folded stack of bills. U.S. Not a lot by our standards. Too much by his.

"You only have to hear this," she said. "You take us to where the fence is low. You wait. You bring back whoever walks out."

His eyes stayed on her face. Not the money. Smart man.

"And if no one comes back?"

"Then you go home," she said. "And you don't ever say our names to anyone who might care."

He took the money. Not because he was reassured. Because he understood his role in this and wanted it to be brief.

"Suban," he muttered. Get on.

The dock creaked under my boots as I stepped down into the boat. My body complained in small, precise ways—the residue of yesterday's collapse clinging to my muscles, the residual strain of dead sunlight still baked into my skin. But Elise's blood ran in me, steady and cold, smoothing the edges. My vision was too sharp. The night wasn't dark; it was layered. Every shadow had gradations.

Bruce climbed in after me, making the boat list. He carried weight like it was an old friend. Samantha followed, then Lacy, Olivia, Elise last. She sat at the bow, one hand on the rim, body angled forward like she could see the island already.

The man untied the rope from the cleat, shoved us off, and jumped in, landing with a practiced sway. He pulled the cord on the motor. It coughed once, twice, then roared to indifferent life.

We slid away from the dock into the mouth of the bay.

The town fell behind us—its few lights smeared into gold lines on the water, then swallowed entirely by the dark. Ahead, the sea opened up. The sky was low with clouds, stars smothered. The only clues that we were moving through anything at all were the slaps of waves against the hull and the occasional phosphorescent flare of something alive below the surface.

No one spoke for a while. Wind tore the words away before they were born.

I watched Elise's profile in the faint spill from the boat's bulb. The night made her face almost featureless, all contour and suggestion, but I knew every line. I knew the exact place her mouth tightened when she was calculating casualties. I knew the set of her jaw when she'd already decided who was going to die.

She felt me looking. Of course she did. Without turning, without raising her voice, she said, "Stop."

"I didn't say anything."

"You're thinking loudly," she said. "You're doing the thing where you assign last words before anyone has earned them."

"I'm trying to guess the part you left out," I said.

She glanced back then, just enough for her eyes to catch the bulb's light. "You're really going to pick that fight now?"

"Time's limited," I said. "Just being efficient."

Her mouth twitched. Not quite a smile. Not tonight.

"We get to the island," she said. "We use the low point. Samantha handles the feeds. Bruce takes point on the ground. Lacy sticks to you. You stick to me. That's the part you already know. Everything else depends on how stupid they are."

"Great," I said.

"That's the best version," she replied. "You don't want the other one."

"What's the other one?"

She turned back to the dark sea. "The one where they're smarter."

The motor droned, a constant throat-sore growl. Spray hit my face and dried almost instantly, salt tightening my skin. My hearing was a burden—every piston movement, every change in wind direction, every shift of weight on the boards cataloged and filed. Beneath it all, under the engine and the slap and the hiss, I could hear six separate heartbeats on the boat.

Five of them were too fast.

Samantha sat opposite me, elbows braced on her knees, fingers tapping a restless pattern against the plastic of her hard case. She met my eyes once, briefly. There was something there I hadn't seen on her before. Not fear. Resignation. The kind that had already been negotiated.

"You okay?" I mouthed.

She rolled her eyes and mouthed back, "Focus."

Lacy was beside her, gaze locked straight ahead, fingers worrying the frayed cuff of his sleeve. The last time I'd seen him like this, he'd had my blood in his throat and panic in his eyes, convinced he was dying. Now his pulse was steady. Faster than mine, but not frantic. Changed, but still so painfully young.

"Never been on a boat before," he muttered, deciding this was the moment to confess.

"You picked a hell of a first time," Bruce rumbled.

He sat near the stern, built out of brick and fatigue. His beard had gone mostly steel since Whitby. He'd shaved it down for travel, but the shadow remained, like stubble on a statue. There was calm written across his shoulders, the kind that said he'd done worse than this more times than he cared to admit. That kind of calm is always a lie.

"You get seasick, kid?" he asked Lacy.

"Fuck off," Lacy said.

Bruce laughed. "Elise?" he called forward. "You know what the policy is for vomit in the boat, right?"

"Kill him and throw him overboard," she said, without turning. "We're not animals."

There was a ripple of almost-laughter. It died quickly, but it was enough to remind me everyone here still understood humor as a concept, not just as a weapon.

The boat veered slightly. Off the port side, a new shape began to form in the dark. At first it was just absence—darkness thicker than the sky, a cutout in the horizon. Then details assembled. The low rise of coastline. Darker lines of trees. A ragged edge of rock where the island's teeth met the sea.

The Island.

The man cut the motor halfway out, letting us drift in on our own inertia. He said something under his breath, something halfway between a prayer and a curse.

"What's that?" Olivia asked.

"He says this is a horrible idea," Elise answered. "So we're in the right place."

Lights winked in the distance along the island's main curve—resorts and houses and bars selling tropical lies. We were headed away from all of that, toward a stretch of coastline that had no lights at all.

A pale line emerged ahead: surf breaking against rock. Beyond it, a darker band that wasn't quite shadow.

Fence.

"You sure about this cut?" Bruce asked.

"Yes," Elise said. "Third inlet past the ruined pier. There's a dip in the ridge. The fence follows the ridge. It's lowered from erosion—they never fixed it."

"You really did your research after all, huh," Samantha said.

Elise didn't answer. She didn't have to.

The boat kissed the rocky coastline with a dull thud. Waves slopped around us, shoving the hull against whatever was underneath us.

He pointed. "Veinte minutos," he said. Twenty minutes. "Then the patrol boat."

"Plenty," Elise said.

He looked like he wanted to argue. He didn't. He reached under the bench, pulled out a coil of rope and tossed one end to Bruce, who caught it with one hand and looped it over a natural hook of stone. The boat held.

"Stay," Elise told the man, in English now. "If this boat isn't here when we get back, I will find you."

He squinted at her, trying to decide if that was bravado or threat or both. Then he nodded, because he'd already been paid.

We climbed out.

The rocks were slick with algae and something unidentifiable. My boots slipped once, skidding, before my reflexes caught up and compensated, weight shifting faster than should have been possible. My body liked this. It liked the dark and the climb and the mission. It liked having something to hunt.

We moved up the natural slope, a broken staircase of boulders and scrub. The island air was thicker than the mainland, heavy with damp sand, rotting plant matter, and the faint underlying tang of chemical discharge that didn't belong to any natural place.

By the time we reached the crest, my shirt clung to me with a film of sweat. It wasn't heat that bothered me. It was the smell.

The fence started a few yards ahead, running along the ridge like a scar. Ten feet high, steel mesh, topped with coils of razor wire that glinted faintly in the distant ambient light from the facility beyond. The posts were sunk deep in concrete. Someone had meant it.

Samantha crouched, set her case down, and popped it open. Inside were cutters, loops of bundled wire, small matte-black devices that hummed softly when she brushed their surfaces.

"Low point's there," she said, nodding toward a section where the ground dipped slightly, the fence bowing with it. "Less ground clearance. Less flex. They think it makes it stronger. It makes it predictable."

She pulled on a pair of thin gloves and went to work. The rest of us fanned out, forming a loose arc along the ridge, watching the facility.

From here I could see it better. Chrome and concrete hunched in the clearing below. A cluster of squat buildings ringed by roadways, all laid out in neat, brutal lines. Floodlights speared the sky, angling outward, sweeping uselessly over empty air. Inside the fences, the lighting was softer—white and sterile and wrong in the middle of an island.

"There," Olivia whispered, pointing.

I followed her finger. A pair of guards walked the inner perimeter, shadows stretching in the floodlight beams. They moved with the bored precision of people who did this every night and had not yet been given a reason to regret it.

"You see dogs?" Bruce asked.

I listened. The wind carried insects, distant engines, the slow grind of a generator. No panting. No chains.

"No," I said.

"And their cameras?" Samantha murmured without looking back.

"Two at the north corner, one at the south," I said. "One on the roof of the main building. Rotating. You'll hate them."

"I always do," she said.

Metal snipped softly. Once. Twice. Samantha's cutters moved fast and efficient, taking out a rectangle in the lower half of the fence. When she finished, she caught the cut edges before they could fall and clatter, easing the piece inward onto the sand beyond. Then she reached into the case and pulled out one of the humming devices, attaching it to the live wire above.

"Looping," she said. "To the system, the fence looks untouched."

"How long?" Elise asked.

"Long enough," Samantha said.

"That's not an answer," I muttered.

"It's the only one I've got," she said. "This isn't their full network. That's deeper in. Out here they're lazy."

There was that word again.

Elise knelt, lifted the bottom of the cut section to test the give, then nodded once. "Bruce. You and I first. Alex, Lacy with us. Olivia, Samantha last. Keep low."

I dropped into a crouch, the world shrinking to the scraped sand under the fence, the cold prickle of cut metal near my neck as I slid through. The smell inside the perimeter changed immediately—less beach, more concrete. The sea fell away behind us, replaced by the hum of infrastructure.

From here, the buildings loomed larger, looming blocks of white and grey. The main structure was a long, low slab with a higher center spine—lab windows along the upper floor, dark at this hour. Off to the right, smaller annexes sprouted from the main like tumors. A parking area sat further off, half full of black SUVs, lights off, engines cooling.

"No alarms," Bruce murmured.

"Yet," Elise replied.

We moved.

Years of security theater had drilled patterns into me—hug walls, count cameras, memorize sight-lines. Here, everything in me was heightened. I could feel the guards' heartbeats even when they passed behind buildings. I could hear the faint jangle of keys on one man's belt, the soft squeak of rubber soles on concrete. The wind shifted every few seconds, bringing with it scents of bleach, burned coffee, sweat, the tang of something metallic and sharp that could only be sterilized blood.

My own hunger stirred, reptilian, curious.

Not now, I told it. Later.

We reached the shadow of the first building, pressed ourselves against the cool concrete. Above, a window glowed faintly with blue light—monitors, server racks, something humming. Samantha brushed past me, her shoulder ghosting mine, and slid under it toward a service door with a keypad.

"This is us," she whispered.

"You sure?" Bruce asked.

"No," she said. "But if I were them and I didn't want anyone seeing how I got in and out, I'd use this one."

She set her case down again, hands already moving, wires out, small tablet lit. Numbers scrolled. The keypad beeped once, red. Twice, red. The third time it chirped green.

"That was fast," I said.

The lock clicked. She pulled the door open an inch. Cool air spilled out, dry and filtered, carrying cleaner versions of the scents I'd picked up outside—bleach, metal, fear.

Elise held up a hand.

"Inside," she said. "We stay tight. No heroics. No detours. We get to the heart, we cut it out, we leave."

"And if it doesn't go that clean?" Bruce asked.

She looked at him, and something passed between them that I wasn't invited to read.

"Then we improvise," she said.

We slipped inside.

The difference was immediate. Outside, the world had been organic, wet, noisy. In here, everything was engineered. The air was conditioned to an indifference that made my skin feel wrong. The lights were recessed, steady and soft, with no flicker. The floor was polished concrete, marked with faint lines where equipment had been moved, cables taped and re-taped. The walls were the same white-grey non-color favored by people who wanted to pretend they were neutral.

We stood in a narrow service corridor. To the left, it turned and branched. To the right, it dead-ended in a closed door marked with a simple red sign: AUTHORIZED PERSONNEL ONLY.

"That's us," Elise said.

"It would be nice if once in my life that were literally true," I muttered.

"Dream smaller," she said.

Samantha moved ahead, tablet out, glancing at a map she'd pulled down before we left. Her brain made a clean geometry of this place. Mine made something else.

"Are you hearing anything?" she asked me.

"Server room above us," I said. "Freezers to the left. Something with pumps to the right. More guards outside than inside. For now."

"Cameras?" Olivia pressed.

"Two in this hallway," I said. "One at each end. They will see us eventually."

Samantha looked up, spotted the black domes in the corner. She pulled another small device from her pack, stuck it to the wall below one. It emitted a barely audible whine and a slow, blinking light.

"Blind," she said. "Three minutes."

"Then we move," Elise said.

We moved.

It almost worked.

We passed two doors, both closed. One smelled like chemicals and metal instruments—storage. The other smelled like nothing at all—probably empty. There were no windows. No signs. People who designed places like this didn't like annotation. They trusted maps and clearance levels and a shared fear of getting lost.

We reached the third door. This one was heavier, with a card reader and a numeric pad and a small lens above it.

"Retinal," Samantha said. "Of course."

"You can get past that?" Lacy whispered.

"Not politely," she said.

I swallowed. "What does impolite look like?"

Before anyone could answer, the overhead lights flickered.

Once. Twice. Then stabilized.

My skin crawled. Every hair on my arms lifted. The hum in the walls shifted frequency, subtly.

"Elise," I said.

"I know," she said.

She'd gone still in the way only she could—every muscle relaxed, every sense flared. She listened to the building listening to us.

"They know we're here," she said.

"How?" Olivia hissed.

Samantha checked her tablet, jaw tightening. "The loop just broke. Someone's watching the peripheral feeds manually. They patched around my spoof."

"They shouldn't have been looking," Elise said. "Not on this side. No one looks here unless—"

And then the alarms started.

It wasn't a single siren. It was a layered assault—low-frequency bass notes that you felt in your bones, higher keening tones meant to disorient, and a mechanical voice calmly instructing everyone to remain where they were while security assessed the situation.

Red lights began to spin along the ceiling, washing the corridor in bloody pulses.

"Well," Bruce said. "Here's your other version."

"What now?" Lacy said, already flattening himself against the wall, eyes wide.

"Now we do it loud," Elise said.

The first bullet hit the door handle two inches from my hand. The impact rang up my arm like a bell. A heartbeat later, the world filled with the sound of automatic fire chewing through drywall.

"Down!" Bruce bellowed.

We dove. Concrete burned along my palms as I hit the floor and rolled, pulling Lacy with me. Chips of wall sprayed overhead. The smell of gunpowder and hot metal burst into the clean lab air, clashing with bleach and refrigerant.

"Back!" Samantha yelled. "There's a cross-corridor—"

"No time," Elise snapped.

I saw it then, the calculation running behind her eyes: distance to cover, number of shooters, angles, what we were versus what they thought we were.

"Alex," she said. "Left side. Take their eyes."

There was no room to argue. Some feral part of me had been waiting for this since we stepped onto the boat.

I moved.

The first guard came through the intersection ahead, gun already up. I saw the moment his brain registered that I was closer than he'd expected, that I wasn't where I should have been. His pupils blew wide.

We slammed into the opposite wall.

Bone gave under my shoulder—his, not mine. His breath bellowed out. My hand closed around his wrist, twisted; the gun clattered free. Another shot went off wild, punching a fluorescent light and showering us both in glass.

My teeth found his throat almost without instruction.

The taste was brutal. Hot. Copper and salt and adrenaline and the sour metallic residue of fear. His life hit my tongue and my body reacted with an obscene gratitude, every nerve lighting, every muscle warming. The world snapped into a clarity that made everything before it look like sleepwalking.

I didn't stop.

A hand fisted in the back of my shirt. Elise yanked me off, hard. My teeth tore free, leaving a ragged hole. Blood sprayed the wall in a fan.

"Leave him, take his gun," she said. "He's done."

The guard slid down the wall, hands pressed uselessly to his neck, red pumping between his fingers.

More boots pounded toward us.

Bruce stepped into the gap, filling the hall with gunfire.

For a moment, the corridor was nothing but muzzle flashes and the low, rhythmic boom of return fire. He wasn't fast the way we were. He was fast the way trained men are—deliberate, controlled. He sighted, squeezed, moved, using every inch of the corridor's geometry, every scrap of cover.

Three men went down before they realized their rounds weren't slowing him.

"Body armor," one of them yelled in English, panicked. "He's—"

He didn't finish the sentence. Bruce's bullet took him in the face.

"Right flank!" Samantha called.

I pivoted. A side door had slammed open while we were focused forward. Two more guards spilled out, but I was already firing. They hit the ground hard.

Olivia moved without hesitation. She went low, sweeping the first man's legs out from under him with a slide kick that looked almost choreographed. As he fell, she grabbed his collar and used his momentum to hurl him into his partner. They hit the opposite wall in a tangle.

Her knife flashed once. Twice.

They stopped moving.

"Clear!" she snapped as she picked up one of their assault rifles.

The alarms wailed on, insistent.

"This is too many, too fast," Samantha yelled over the noise. "They were waiting."

"For you?" I asked Elise.

"For us," she said. "For any of us."

She grabbed the fallen guard's body and hauled it toward the retinal door.

"Samantha!" she barked.

Samantha was already there, yanking the man's head up by his hair, shoving his face toward the lens. The little light above it flicked from red to green. The lock thunked.

"Inside," Elise said. "Move."

We poured through the door into a wider corridor, this one lined with glass on one side. Behind it, rooms stretched away, lit with sterile brightness. I saw lab benches, arrays of equipment, refrigeration units. In one room, a row of stainless-steel chairs with restraints. In another, tanks.

Most of them were empty.

Some weren't.

Figures floated in viscous liquid—human shapes, distorted by the curve of glass and fluid. Tubes ran into their arms, their throats. Some had hair that drifted around their faces like seaweed. Others were bald, marked with surgical lines.

The hunger inside me recoiled. This blood was wrong. Tainted.

"MIR-4476 trials," Samantha said, voice flat. "Human stage."

Lacy choked out a half-formed curse. Olivia's face went blank. Bruce didn't look at the tanks at all. His eyes were on the far end of the corridor, where another door waited. Bigger. Heavier. No glass panel. Only another reader and a keypad.

"That's the lab," Elise said.

"How many doors between us and their core?" I asked.

"Two," Samantha said. "This one, then the inner. That's the one I can't spoof from outside. We need a live hand."

Another flicker in the lights. Another subtle shift in the hum. My teeth buzzed.

"What is that?" I asked.

"Generators cycling," Samantha said. "They're routing power. Locking down sections. We're in a moving maze."

"We stand still, we die," Bruce said. "We go forward, we might not."

"There's a motivational poster in there somewhere," I said.

"Shut up," Elise said, but there was no heat in it. Just focus. Her eyes tracked the ceiling, counting sensors, sprinklers, vents.

The keypad beeped suddenly, unprompted. A red bar slid across a tiny display.

LOCKDOWN ENGAGED, it read.

"Well," Samantha said. "That's bad."

"How bad?" Lacy asked.

"Inside, okay," she said. "Outside, trapped. They just sealed the peripheral doors. Our quiet exit is gone."

"So we make a loud one," Bruce said.

He slung his rifle, shrugged his pack off one shoulder, and dug inside. When his hand came out, it held a compact charge. It looked like C4, but I wasn't sure. He slapped it against the wall near the lab door, pressed it into place, and unfolded a small, wired detonator.

"Someone's been shopping," I said.

"I keep hobbies," he said. "Back."

We stepped away, putting as much hallway between us and the charge as we could without losing sight of the corners. The tanks watched us with their helpless drifting.

"Three," Bruce said calmly. "Two. One."

The blast hit like a giant's fist. The wall bucked, concrete shattering inward. Glass exploded, knifing down the corridor. The air slapped my face hot, then rushed out in its own kind of scream. The alarms shifted up a register, offended.

When the dust cleared enough to see, the door was no longer a door. It was twisted metal and ragged edges. Beyond it, a dark opening yawned.

"That's your entry," Bruce said. "Go."

We didn't get to.

The first tear gas canister clanged off the floor near Olivia's feet.

She swore, kicking it instinctively. It spun away, trailing white smoke. Another came from the opposite direction, bouncing, rolling.

"Back!" Samantha yelled. "Masks—"

"We don't have masks," Lacy coughed.

"Hold your breath," Elise snapped. "Stay low."

I didn't breathe. The gas was still assaultive—stinging eyes, burning skin, coating the inside of my nose with chemical bitterness. I heard human lungs catch and wheeze behind me.

Boots thundered from both ends of the corridor.

"Split up," Elise said. "Bruce with me, left. Samantha, right with Olivia. Alex—"

"I'm with you," I said.

"No," she said. "You're with Lacy."

It wasn't a request. It hit like a shove.

There was no time to argue. There was no time for anything. The first wave of guards came through the gas like they were born in it. Full tactical gear, masks, goggles, rifles up—every one of them bleeding that same wrong purple around their bodies. These weren't the bored perimeter guards. These were the ones they called when they wanted something ugly cleaned up.

Bruce yelled and met them head-on.

He didn't look like a man then. He looked like a breach given shape. He grabbed the barrel of the nearest gun and wrenched, dragging its owner bodily toward him. His free hand clamped on the man's helmet, twisted. Something crunched. The man went down. Bruce turned the stolen rifle on the second.

Shots burst, deafening in the enclosed space. One guard slammed into a tank, spiderwebbing the glass. Liquid began to leak in slow, thick sheets.

"Alex!" Elise's voice cut through everything. "Go!"

She was already moving, a blur of grey and intent. She wove through the gas and gunfire, every step placed where it needed to be a fraction before the bullets chewed the air she'd been in. She hit the cluster at the left end low, taking one man's knee backward, then rising with inhuman speed to drive her elbow into another's throat. There was a choreography to it, a brutal grace.

I wanted to be beside her.

Instead, I grabbed Lacy's arm and dragged him toward the broken door, toward the blasted opening into the inner zones.

"We can't leave them," he choked.

"We're not," I lied. "We're following the plan."

"This wasn't the plan," he said, blood already seeping from a cut above his brow where shrapnel had caught him.

"No," I said. "This is the improvisation."

Behind us, Samantha had peeled right with Olivia, using the leaking gas as cover. She tossed one of her humming devices down the corridor. A second later, the overhead sprinklers erupted, dumping cold water onto everything. The gas thinned, swirling. The guards' visors fogged.

"We can't see shit," a muffled voice shouted through a mask.

"That's the point," Samantha muttered.

She darted forward, hand flashing. For a moment I thought she was throwing a knife. It was something smaller, flatter—some sort of explosive. She slapped it onto the side of one man's rifle. It sparked, then detonated in a contained blast that shredded the weapon and took half his hand with it.

His scream cut through the alarms.

The others pivoted toward her, guns tracking.

"Sam!" Bruce bellowed.

He was too far. Too many bodies between them. Elise saw it first, her eyes flicking, calculation slamming into inevitability.

"Samantha!" she shouted. "Down!"

Samantha looked back, over her shoulder, just for a second. Our eyes met.

There was no surprise in hers. Just a tired sort of satisfaction.

"Go," she mouthed.

Then the world tore open around her.

The guards' return fire was disciplined, tight grouping. Center mass. They treated her like what she was—an enemy asset, not a woman. Bullets slammed into her chest, her stomach, her shoulder. The impact lifted her off her feet and threw her back against the glass of another tank.

For a heartbeat, she stayed there, pinned against it like a specimen. Cracks spread from behind her, radiating out. Blood smeared the glass.

Then both she and the tank gave way.

Water avalanched into the corridor, washing bodies and rubble toward us. Something pale and half-grown rolled out with it, a failed attempt at a person. It hit the floor with a sick sound.

"Samantha!" Lacy screamed.

I grabbed him harder, dragging him through the rising water toward the breached doorway. My muscles burned with effort, not because I was weak, but because everything in me wanted to turn back and tear the men who'd shot her into pieces.

A hand clamped on my arm, iron-strong. Bruce.

He'd fought his way backward toward us, covering Elise's retreat in bursts of disciplined fire. His left arm hung wrong, blood leaking from under his sleeve where something had torn through muscle. His face was gaunt, pale.

"Get him inside," he said, jerking his chin toward Lacy. "Get to the inner door. You know what you have to do."

"How?" I said. "We need Samantha—"

"You have me," he said.

Another wave of guards hit the far end of the corridor, pushing through the water and gas, stepping over their dead. A deeper alarm began to sound—I recognized the pitch. External response. They'd called someone.

"Bruce," Elise said.

Their eyes met. A conversation happened in the space between them that had nothing to do with words.

"I'll hold this hall," he said. "You finish what you came for."

"You don't have to—" I started.

"Yes," he said. "I do. This was always the way it was going to end for me. Better here than in that house, waiting for them to come."

He shoved me hard toward the breach. My heels slid on wet concrete. Lacy stumbled with me.

"Alex," Elise said, voice very quiet in the chaos. "Listen to me."

I snapped to her like a magnet.

"You keep him alive," she said, nodding at Lacy. "Stick to the plan. You don't come back out until you see my face or the sky. Is that clear?"

"Bruce—"

"Is already dead," she said. "He just gets to decide how."

It was cruel. It was merciful. It was true.

Bruce grinned, teeth white in his blood-smeared beard. "Try to make it worth it, yeah?" he said. "I'd hate to die for nothing."

Then he turned away from us, squaring his shoulders, stepping into the mouth of the corridor like it was a doorway to something he'd been walking toward for years.

He braced his feet against the slick floor, raised his rifle, and became a wall.

"Go!" he roared.

We went.

The blasted doorway tore skin off my shoulder as I shoved Lacy through ahead of me. Shards of concrete and twisted metal clawed at my clothes. The world beyond was dimmer, lit only by emergency strips along the floor. The air here was cooler, drier. The alarms were muffled.

Behind us, Bruce's gun thundered. The returning fire

was a constant metallic snarl. Somewhere amid it, he laughed. A deep, rolling sound that cut through even the machinery of death.

It stopped.

Not all at once. First the laughter, then the gunfire, staggered. Then nothing from his end but the continuing wail of the building.

Lacy sagged. I held him up.

"We can't—" he started.

"We will," I said. My voice sounded like someone else's. "We don't get to waste him."

Elise crawled through the breach after us, blood on her cheek that wasn't hers. Olivia followed, panting, one arm pressed to her ribs. There was too much red on her fingers.

"You hit?" I asked.

"Grazed," she said. "They're worse."

Through the gap we'd just come from, I glimpsed a heap of bodies in tactical gear, floating in the water tinged pink. Among them, bigger, more still, was Bruce.

Elise pulled herself to her feet like the wound was somewhere she refused to acknowledge. She didn't look back.

"Roll call," she said. "Samantha?"

Silence answered her.

Something cracked in the air around us. Not sound. Pressure.

Elise's jaw clenched. For a second, her eyes closed. When she opened them, they were colder.

"Four," she said. "That's what we have. Four is enough."

"You knew," I said. I couldn't stop it. The accusation pushed its way out. "This. Them. You saw this version."

"I saw every version," she said. "This is the one where

you live long enough to hate me properly. We don't have time to litigate it."

There it was. The cost she'd hidden. Paid in full—in blood.

The corridor here was narrower, lined with smooth, uninterrupted walls. The floor strips glowed a dim blue-white, leading us deeper. Ahead, at the far end, waited another door. This one was worse than the last—no visible handle, no keypad, just a seamless panel broken only by a small black square at shoulder height.

"Inner lock," Samantha had called it. "Biometric and code. Needs a live hand."

We'd just lost the only one who knew how to bypass it.

"Now what?" Lacy asked. His voice had gone thin around the edges. "We're trapped."

"No," Elise said. "We're committed."

She stepped up to the panel, studying it. The building hummed nervously around us, rerouting, adjusting, like a body reacting to an infection.

Olivia leaned back against the wall, breathing hard, eyes closed for a count of three. When she opened them, she was steady again.

"You hear anyone?" she asked me.

I listened.

The facility's outer layers were a storm—footsteps pounding, muffled shouts, radios, the clatter of equipment. Here, closer to the heart, it was quieter. I heard the steady whir of cooling systems, the rush of water through pipes. Behind the door, faintly, a cluster of softer sounds—typing, the scrape of a chair, a heart beating faster than it should in a man who thought he was safe.

"One," I said. "Maybe two. Not many. They think this door is enough."

"Arrogant," Elise murmured. "Convenient."

She turned to us. Her hair clung damply to her forehead. There was water on her lashes, not tears.

"This is the line," she said. "Past this, there's no graceful exit. No surrender that keeps you breathing. We get in, we break what we came to break, we walk out over whatever's left. If you want to go back, you go now."

"There's nothing to go back to," Olivia said.

"Same," Lacy whispered.

I didn't answer. I stepped up beside her, shoulder touching hers, the contact small and absolute.

"You already know," I said. "You told me last night. This is the war you made for me. I don't get to flinch now."

A tiny muscle jumped at the corner of her mouth. The confession between us from the motel bed hung here too, invisible but heavy.

"Good," she said. "Because I'm out of backup plans."

She placed her palm flat against the black square.

For a second, nothing happened. Then a beam of red light scanned her hand, up and down, tracing bone structure, vein pattern. The square blinked.

"ACCESS DENIED," a calm synthetic voice said. "UNREGISTERED PROFILE."

"Elise Quinn," she said, looking directly at the panel. "Override. Code black."

There was a pause. Somewhere deep in the walls, something spun up—a deeper processor, an older failsafe. The square flickered.

"VOICEPRINT MATCH," it said. "OVERRIDE REQUIRES SECONDARY AUTHORIZATION."

"Of course it does," she said under her breath.

She turned her head slightly, looking through me. For a second, I thought she was staring at nothing. Then I realized she was looking through the wall, through floors and corridors, to wherever Samantha's body lay.

"Secondary authorization: Samantha Reyes," she said quietly. "Fail-safe clause. In the event of asset loss, transfer authorization to first-tier field lead present at time of breach. Confirm."

The panel was silent. The building hummed, thinking.

"CONFIRMED," it said.

The strip above the door flipped from red to green. Locks unseated inside the walls with a cascading clunk.

Air hissed.

The door began to slide open.

The hum from within was deeper, heavier, full of machines that thought they were important.

Beyond the threshold, I saw the edge of a vast room—steel and glass and cables, monitors casting blue light over banks of equipment. This was the lab. The real one. The place where they'd pulled Morbus Sanguiatis apart and tried to rebuild it into something they could sell.

Elise looked at me. Not like a weapon. Not like an asset. Like the man she had just chosen to ruin and keep.

"You ready?" she asked.

"No," I said. "Do it anyway."

A man's voice drifted out of the lab, steady, familiar, far too comfortable with the shape of her name.

"Elise?"

Lacy, Olivia, and I all turned toward her in the same breath—waiting, trusting, bracing.

She didn't turn.

She didn't even blink.

And in the cold wash of the doorway's light, I finally saw it—the smallest shift in her expression, a fracture in the mask, there and gone—the kind of look a person wore right before they stepped neatly out of the blast radius.

# CHAPTER 15
# NOBODY'S NOTHING AFTER ALL

Elise stepped forward.

Not toward me. Toward the voice.

"Dr. Torres," she said.

My stomach flipped. Not at the name—at the way she said it. No surprise. No question mark. Just greeting.

The man stepped into view from behind a bank of monitors like he'd been waiting for his cue. Late fifties. White coat over dark clothes. Brown skin. Close-cut hair gone silver at the temples. Eyes like scalpel steel. No badge. No theatrics. Just the quiet confidence of someone standing in his own lungs.

"Elise," he said again, softer. "You made it."

Behind him, the lab stepped down in concentric rings—equipment circling a central well. Glass, steel, cables bundled in black trunks, machines humming with the kind of power that never saw daylight. Blue monitor light washed over his shoulders, the walls, the side of Elise's face.

Olivia swore under her breath. Lacy just froze, his hand finding my sleeve.

"Who the fuck is that?" he whispered.

I didn't answer. My throat had gone dry.

Elise didn't turn. "You locked the outer rings faster than we modeled," she said to Torres. "That was sloppy."

He smiled a little. "You're alive, aren't you? Outcome's acceptable."

"Not for them," I said.

He looked at me then, really looked, and it was like being cataloged. Not as a person. As inventory.

"Alexander Hopes," he said. "Finally."

My full name sounded wrong in his mouth. Like he was reading the label on a specimen jar.

"Stop," I said to Elise, and I heard my own voice break. "Whatever this is. Stop."

She exhaled slowly. Then she turned.

There are moments in a life when the floor doesn't fall away so much as reveal it was never there. This was one of them.

Her face was calm. Not cold, not blank. Worse. Resolved.

"This is it," she said. "The heart."

"Of the lab?" I asked. "Or the lie?"

Lacy shifted closer, shoulders touching mine. Olivia's gun stayed up, barrel cutting the space between Elise and Torres, trying to frame a world that made sense.

"Explain," Olivia said. "Now."

Torres lifted his hands a little—not surrender, just irritation. "Are we really doing this part?" he asked Elise. "You're inside the inner ring. They're exhausted, bleeding. We have—"

"We have time," she said.

Something in the way she said we made my skin crawl.

Behind us, the door finished closing with a soft, final hiss. The seam vanished. No handle. No reader. Just wall.

Lacy jolted. "Elise—"

"I know," she said. "I locked it."

"You what?" Olivia's voice snapped sharp. "What the hell does that mean?"

"It means there's no going back the way we came," Elise said. "There never was, not really. You knew that when you stepped on the boat. I asked each of you if you wanted to turn back—you didn't. You had a choice. This is it."

"That's fucking bullshit," I said.

Her eyes met mine. For a second I saw her—the woman who'd pressed my forehead to hers in a motel room and promised there was a version where we lived. The woman who'd dragged me out of a burning harbor and put her blood in my veins because she refused to let me die.

Then it slipped. Or maybe it had never been there.

"You remember the first time you saw it," she said quietly. "In Whitby."

I blinked. "Saw what?"

"Color," she said. "Around people. You told yourself it was an aftereffect. Head trauma. Stress. You told yourself it would fade."

It hadn't. If anything, it had sharpened. Guards haloed in that wrong bloom of purple. The violent streaked with red. The unblooded wearing white they didn't know they carried.

"I told you there were three auras—white, red, purple," she went on. "And that once you had the gene in your blood, you stopped casting one."

"And," I said. "You told me—"

"What I didn't tell you," she cut in, "is that there's a fourth. Pink."

My heart stuttered.

"You know who has that aura?" she asked.

"Who?" I shouted.

"Only one person in the world—well, two now. Me and you."

Silence hit harder than any sound.

"Why did you think everyone else with the gene follows me?" she said. "Why did you think I'm the one they're afraid of?"

"You said carriers don't cast," I said. "You said when the gene's active—"

"I lied," she said.

The word hit harder than any bullet.

Torres watched with clinical interest, like this was the part of the trial where the subject realizes the restraints.

"Every carrier of the gene sees the auras but doesn't cast one," she said. "I'm the only one who ever did. Pink. It's why they fear me. You and I are the only ones with the full pink spectrum. That's why you always felt stared at. People look at you the way they look at me. They just don't know why."

Lacy's hand tightened on my sleeve. Olivia swallowed hard.

I looked at them both. "Why didn't either of you tell me?"

Olivia's answer was fast, defensive. "Elise said we couldn't. We didn't have a choice."

"Get to the part where you locked us in a murder basement with your pet scientist," Olivia said. "We're bleeding out on exposition here."

Elise's mouth twitched—not with humor. With irritation at being rushed.

She stepped closer to me. The lab's light striped her

face, picking out the fine sheen of sweat on her skin, the smear of someone else's blood on her cheek.

"You always wanted it to mean something," she said. "The book. The prize. The interviews. You wanted all of it to be proof that you weren't just...chance. That the world made sense if you could stack enough pages on one side of the scale. I've spent centuries looking for another person with my aura. I never found anyone. And then you wrote yourself right into my orbit."

"Congratulations," I said. "What the fuck? And why is that lab coat undressing me with his eyes?"

Torres chuckled. "He's charming," he said.

"Fuck yourself," I snapped.

Elise didn't look at me. "You weren't chance," she said. "You never were. You're the only living human who had both the original Morbus Sanguiatis gene and the synthetic derivative active in your system without full conversion. You survived two architectures fighting over the same body and didn't tear apart. You wrote about it like a monster story because you didn't have language for what it was."

My heart thudded once, loud in my ears.

"What it was—what it is," Torres said, stepping in, "is proof of concept. Stability. Reversibility. A key."

I shook my head. "No. I'm just another mistake you people made."

"I made you," Elise snapped.

"Every breakthrough is a mistake executed correctly," he said. "You're the one that stuck."

Elise was closer now, close enough that I could see the tiny scar at her jawline where a blade had nearly taken her throat.

"I've spent my entire life like this," she said. "Hearing other people's hearts, smelling their fear, reading the colors they don't even know they wear. I've outlived friends. Lovers. Teams. My family. I've watched humans crash through their small lives in straight lines and burn out, and I've stayed exactly the same. Do you have any idea what that does to a person?"

"Yeah," I said. "It turns them into you."

"Into someone who understands cost," she said. "That there is no change without it."

"Say what you're saying," Olivia said. "Stop playing with it."

Elise looked at her almost gently. "You think you wouldn't make the same choice?" she asked. "If someone offered you another life? One where you weren't born into someone else's nightmare? Where your body was really yours?"

"Yeah," Olivia said. "I would. The difference is I wouldn't sell out my people to get it."

Elise held her gaze for a moment. Then she sighed.

The gun was in her hand before my brain caught up to the movement.

One shot.

A dark hole bloomed in the center of Olivia's forehead and she dropped like a string had been cut.

"Jesus Christ!" I choked.

Lacy lunged forward. Another shot.

He hit the floor beside her, limbs folding under him, eyes still wide.

"I told you," Elise said to me, not looking away from their bodies. "There were versions."

My chest seized. "Why did you kill them? What the fuck did you do?"

"I did them a favor," she said. "I freed them. From the gene. From me. From all of this."

"Elise…" I said.

"In all of them, you end up here," she said. "That's the fixed point. You were always going to be in this room, on that table."

She nodded past me.

I followed her gaze.

At the center of the lab, sunk slightly into the floor, was a platform. Not a horror-movie slab. Sleek. Narrow. Contoured for a body. Straps coiled at the sides like sleeping snakes. Above it, articulated arms branched from a suspended frame—needles, scanners, instruments whose purpose didn't need names to be terrifying.

My legs went cold.

"Don't," I said.

Her eyes came back to mine. Softened. That was somehow worse.

"You're the only one with a stable dual profile," she said quietly. "You're proof the gene can be toggled without killing the host. To them, you're not a person. You're an interface."

"And to you?" I asked.

She didn't answer.

Torres checked an old analog watch that looked too elegant for this room. "We're at the point where I start the sedation regardless," he said. "We have incoming assets en route."

"I'll handle it," she said.

The words were casual. The weight wasn't.

She faced me fully.

"You wanted the truth," she said. "Here it is: there are only two people in the world whose auras are pink. You were never grateful for your life. I was never given a chance at one. I love you—but I need this. I need to know what it's like to be alive."

The word sounded wrong in her mouth. Small. Human.

"Origin," Torres said from behind her. "And solution."

"You're delaying," he added.

"Shut the fuck up," she snapped, eyes never leaving mine. "We have a deal."

My skin crawled. "We have a deal," I said. "You and me."

"This place was never built to let us walk out," she said. "Their plan from the beginning was to kill everyone who came in here except you and me. They wanted my compliance and your body. No witnesses. No loose ends."

"Sounds tidy," Torres said. "You complicated it."

"I always do," she said.

My hands curled into fists. "So bring the ceiling down," I said. "Fry their servers. Kill Torres. We adapt. We've done it all night."

Her eyes softened for half a breath at the word we. Then hardened again.

"You don't get it," she said. "Of course you don't. You're too selfish. Too wrapped up in yourself."

"How the hell am I the selfish one?" I demanded.

"Because I've watched you," she said. "Every time we walk into a room like this, there are branches. Most people never hear them. I do. All of them. All the ways I can lose the people I bring. It never stops. It has eaten me alive for longer than your entire bloodline has existed."

She tapped her temple. "That's what the gene does to me. It shows me every way I can lose, and demands I pick one. And this time, I'm picking me."

Her gaze slid away, then back. "Maybe I'm tired," she said. "Maybe I'm selfish. Maybe I'm everything you'd call me if you live long enough. But I'm done pretending there's a version where I walk back out into the world and keep doing this forever."

There it was. The real thing.

"You want out," I said.

She nodded, small and final. "I need a way out. You are that. Torres can take it out of me. Not just suppress it. Remove it. Strip the gene from every cell, reseed my marrow, rewire the architecture. He can take this disorder away. He can fix me. You can't. You can only love me—a person you don't even know. I hate you for that."

Torres's smile was thin and satisfied. "We can approximate it," he said. "There will be side effects. Memory loss. Physical adjustment. Identity drift. Nothing we can't quantify."

Elise looked at him then, really looked, and I finally saw how young she still was under all that history. How much he knew it. How much she loathed needing him.

Guards appeared at the edges of my vision, like the lab was growing teeth. Black uniforms, rifles low, faces behind visors. They ringed the room, careful not to step into Elise's immediate orbit.

"You see?" Torres said. "The longer we wait, the more variables we introduce."

Elise stepped back, just enough to be out of reach. Of me. Of them.

"Alex," she said.

My name in her mouth had always been both promise and warning. Now it was something worse.

"You were handed everything," she said. "Talent. Attention. A life people kill for. And you spent it trying to find ways out of yourself. Numbing. Drinking. Hiding in work.

Calling it art when it was just running in circles with better lighting."

The words hit harder than the bullets.

"You think I didn't read you before Whitby?" she asked. "Did you think I didn't watch the interviews, the documentary, the speeches about authenticity while you stayed three drinks deep just to feel tolerable? You had a life. A human, fragile, ordinary life. And you threw it away chasing a bigger monster so you didn't have to look at yourself."

"You were there," I said. "You saw what Cirgenix did. You saw what they turned people into."

"So did you," she said. "And you kept feeding it. Every time you said yes to another adaptation, another reprint, another stage, you made yourself a louder target. You painted a bullseye on your own existence and called it purpose."

Her eyes burned—not with contempt, but with something like envy.

"I have never had the option of being ordinary," she said. "I have never been allowed to fail quietly. Or get tired. Or stop. I have carried this in my veins since the first man in armor tried to burn my village for being 'unnatural.' I have watched centuries of people like you—brilliant, gifted, careless—waste lives I would have killed for."

"And now you are," I said.

She flinched. Once.

"I resent you," she said. "For having what I never did. For wasting it. For being the key to a door you didn't know existed while I've been clawing at walls. I resent you for making me need you."

Her voice cracked on the last word.

I loved her. I hated her. Both sat in my chest like twin rounds, lodged too deep to dig out.

"They were always going to die," she said, glancing at the bodies. "Here, on the island, on another run. That's what we are. We're the space between headlines. The unnamed sources and the bodies that don't make the report. This way, I can make it fast."

"Don't dress it up as mercy," I said. "Don't you dare."

"It is mercy," she said, heat finally bleeding into her tone. "You think they wanted to be taken alive? You think they wanted whatever's waiting in these walls if I said no?"

Torres shrugged. "We have protocols."

"Exactly," she said. "I've seen your protocols."

"I don't know anything," I said. "I thought I did. I thought you—"

"Loved you?" she finished.

I looked at her. Bloody. Beautiful. Monster. Savior. Executioner. My everything.

"Do you?" I asked.

She swallowed. "Yes."

It didn't help.

Guards moved in, boots shifting around the spreading pool of blood. Two of them took me by the arms—not rough, not gentle. Professional. I could have broken their grip. Gone for their throats, their rifles, their eyes. I could have sprinted for Elise and tried to tear her apart the way I had the guard in the corridor.

I didn't move.

It would have meant stepping over Lacy.

"Don't sedate him yet," Torres said. "I want his system clean for baseline readings. Secure him first."

They led me toward the table.

My legs worked. My heart hammered. My mind ran

circles around a single point: Olivia's body, face slack. Lacy's hand still stretched toward the woman who'd killed him.

"Look at me," Elise said.

I didn't.

"Alex," she said. "Please."

The please did it. It always had.

I looked.

She'd given up the gun. Her hands were empty now. That was worse than seeing the weapon.

"You were always going to end up here," she said quietly. "The only variable was who walked you to the table and what they did to you once you were on it."

"That's the story you tell yourself so you can sleep," I said.

"I don't sleep," she said. "Not without you… but with the gene gone, maybe I will."

The guards eased me down onto the metal. It cupped my spine, shoulder blades, calves. Cold. Slightly tacky with disinfectant. I smelled iodine and stainless steel.

Dr. Torres looked to me. "Undress. Everything. Or we will do it for you."

So I did, never taking my eyes off of Elise. Wanting her to watch me, watch what she made me. Watch me die inside. Witness the shame of my nakedness and see that I wasn't scared. That I wasn't fighting it. For her, because of her.

Straps came next, fast and practiced. Over my wrists, biceps, chest, thighs, ankles. Not so tight I couldn't breathe. Just tight enough I couldn't do anything that mattered.

I let them. Every second I didn't fight was another second nobody put a bullet in my head.

Coward, something in me whispered.

Love, something else said.

Torres appeared at the edge of my vision, adjusting an IV line, checking monitors. Up close, the calm cracked; there was a faint tremor in his hands.

"We'll start with a local," he said, almost conversational. "Keep your mind clear as long as possible. The data's cleaner. You might feel pressure. Heat. Don't be dramatic."

"Go fuck yourself," I said.

He smiled thinly. "You writers. Always need the last line. Oh—take that off of him as well." He looked to my watch. A guard made his way over to me.

Elise stopped him. "Wait. I will take it. It's mine. What did you say about this, Alex?"

A rhetorical question she answered herself. "It reminds you of the impermanence of life... this watch existed long before you did. It's seen lives you will never know, stories you will never be a part of. Whoever owned it before you, they lived completely separate lives and now it's mine... for a while, at least. We're connected without ever even knowing that each other existed. It reminds you that you're just a guest here. One day, you'll be gone too, and this watch will keep ticking, winding itself on someone else's wrist. It's a reminder that you're impermanent—just flesh and blood in a world that keeps spinning long after you're gone."

She unclasped it from my wrist, looked at it briefly just before putting it on. "You were talking about me—and you didn't even know it. You were talking about us."

His attention slid off me like I wasn't the center of this. It landed on Elise.

"You understand," he said, "once we begin, there's no reversing the protocol. We re-sequence him, map the toggling function, extract what we need for your procedure. After that, his survival is... not guaranteed."

My breath stuttered.

Elise's jaw flexed. The pink around her burned brighter, furious and terrified. I'd never seen it before. Now I did, and nothing about it made sense.

"You promised he'd live," she said.

"I promised he'd be a priority for as long as he was useful," Torres said. "He will be. After that, I make no guarantees. That's the best anyone gets—I'm not God. I'm a doctor."

"Then you're not touching him," she said.

The room went still.

Torres's mouth thinned. "You think you have leverage?" he asked. "You're an asset with a diminishing shelf life. I'm the only one who can take your burden away. If you walk, you go back to running. Back to hiding. Back to bleeding out teams of children on missions like this until someone less patient than me drops you into a furnace and calls it the same mercy you just showed us."

"I've heard worse careers," she said. The words were almost flippant. The shake underneath wasn't.

She looked at me again.

"This is the only version where I get free," she said. "The only one where you live long enough that your work means something. The data we pull off you will change everything. It's something bigger than me, bigger than all of us."

"You're selling me as a miracle," I said. "That doesn't make you less of a traitor."

Tears pooled in her eyes, bright and furious. She blinked them back like they offended her.

"I know what I am," she said. "I always have. That's the difference between us."

"Why here?" I asked. "Why now? Why not hand me over in Whitby, at the motel, on the boat? Why drag Bruce and Samantha and Olivia and Lacy all the way here just to gun them down on the floor?"

Her nostrils flared. "Because the original plan was for Torres's men to kill them all," she said. "Slow. Messy. Experimental. They wanted to see what my people could take. How long they'd last. What we'd do when you started tearing yourself apart. I changed it. I forced the engagement inside the ring where I could control it. I made it so we didn't have to keep running until they caught and tortured us all. I did this for you, for everyone. It's what's best… it's what's right."

I stared at the bodies. "You call this right? Who are you to determine all of our fates?"

"They died fast," she said. "They died fighting. They died in a place that matters. And they died knowing exactly who killed them."

"That supposed to be comforting?" I asked.

"No, it's supposed to be honest," she said.

Torres cleared his throat, impatient. "Enough," he said. "We begin now, or the next team through that door will be the board, and they don't negotiate with assets. They dissect them."

Elise's fingers flexed at her sides. She drew one slow breath. Another.

Then she leaned over me, blocking out the lab, the guards, Torres. Just her and me, like in motel lamplight and dashboard glow and every stolen hour that started this.

Her hair fell around my cheeks. I could smell smoke, blood, salt.

"I am sorry," she said.

"You're not," I said. "You're relieved."

She didn't argue.

"You always wanted a story that meant something," she said. "This is it. You're not just a man who wrote about monsters. You're the reason they don't get to own the dark forever."

"I'd have settled for finishing a second book," I said.

She almost smiled. "That's your problem—you can't ever settle. It's never enough."

Something cold slid into the back of my hand. Tape pressed down. The sharp sting of a needle seating in a vein. Torres murmuring approval.

"Elise," I said. "Look at me."

"I am," she said.

"Really look," I said. "Because this is the last time you see the man who would've burned the world down for you and still asked what you wanted to build on the ashes."

Her lips parted. For a second, I thought she'd flinch. Run. Shoot Torres. Rip the straps. Choose any other version.

She leaned down further to my face. "I'm sorry. That's the thing though," she said quietly. "You keep talking like this is about me choosing between loving you and loving my own life. It's not. I chose both. That's the sin you'll never forgive."

"If I live long enough to," I said.

She bent and pressed her mouth to my forehead. Not my lips. Not this time. A blessing. A curse.

"I do love you," she whispered.

"Prove it," I said.

She straightened. That tiny fracture I'd seen in her expression at the door sealed over. Whatever was left of

Elise, the woman, stepped back. Elise, the thing this place had been built to contain, remained.

Torres made a small signal. A guard moved to the control panel. The frame above me whirred, positioning itself. Metal arms unfolded, lenses dilating, needles catching sterile light.

"Begin," Torres said.

The machine's hum deepened. A cool burn started in my hand and raced up my arm like frost. My limbs went heavy. Not numb. Just... farther away.

"Elise," I said again. It came out thick. "Don't... leave me."

She stepped back.

That hurt more than the needle.

The guards parted for her. She walked toward the door on the far side of the lab—the one with the observation window. The one that would take her to whatever twisted baptism Torres had promised.

She reached it. The guard there looked to Torres, got a nod, opened it.

She stepped through.

On the other side of the glass, she turned.

We looked at each other across the distance. Metal, light, bodies between us. My world narrowed to that rectangle: her face framed in it, eyes wide, jaw tight, hands clenched at her sides.

I could feel my heart slowing. Each beat a deliberate choice. The machines around me chattered in a language I didn't speak.

Torres said something about baselines. About compatibility. About miracles.

I didn't listen.

I watched Elise watching me.

She lifted her hand and pressed her palm flat to the glass.

"Make it worth it," she mouthed.

The door behind her began to slide shut.

I could taste the medication injected into me, sour, sweet—nauseating.

Then the door sealed.

Everything began to drift to black, erasing the shape of her on the other side of the glass, perfectly placed, perfectly safe.

"Elise..."

# ALSO BY ALEX BROWN

Tomorrow's Train

"I love the way he connected the story together and the insight was amazing."

—**Amazon Reader Review**

ISBN: 978-1-961763-12-8 - (Hardcover)

ISBN: 978-1-961763-13-5 - (Paperback)

ISBN: 978-1-961763-14-2 - (EBook)

# ALSO BY ALEX BROWN

**It Watched Me**

"If Stephen King wrote historical fiction, you might get something like It Watched Me. I was off balance and captivated throughout. Spellbindingly written, this novel was unlike anything else I've read, and I read a lot. 5 stars."

*-Amazon Reader Review*

ISBN 978-1-7377362-0-2 (Paperback

ISBN 978-1-7377362-1-9 (Ebook)

ISBN 978-1-7377362-2-6 (Hardcover)

# ALSO BY ALEX BROWN

### King of Nothing

"An engaging, impassioned, frenzied tale of a comedian on the way up facing thorny challenges."

*-Kirkus Reviews*

2024 Anniversary Edition ISBN: 978-1-961763-07-4

Hardcover ISBN: 978-1737736233

Paperback ISBN: 9798676682361

EBook ASIN: B08G91ZJVH

# ALSO BY ALEX BROWN

Words are Snakes with Arms: A Year in Poems

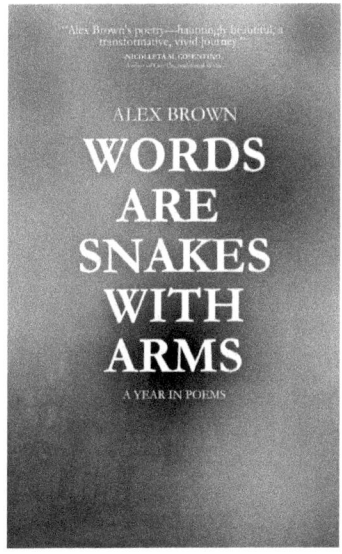

ISBN 978-1-961763-08-1 - (Hardcover)

ISBN: 978-1-961763-09-8 - (Paperback)

ISBN: 978-1-961763-10-4 - (EBook)

www.ingramcontent.com/pod-product-compliance
Lightning Source LLC
LaVergne TN
LVHW012041070526
838202LV00056B/5552